Mobsters and Lobsters

A Hooked & Cooked Cozy Mystery Series

by Lyndsey Cole

is not authorized, associated with, or sponsored by the trademark owners.

Connect with me:

Lyndsey@LyndseyColeBooks.com

www.facebook.com/LyndseyColeAuthor

CONTENTS

Chapter 1

Hannah Holiday took a deep breath and began counting. She only managed to make it to four before words flew from her mouth at the building inspector. "Are you crazy? I've got a big opening planned this weekend for the renovated snack bar. That's in three days." She held up three fingers right in front of his face.

The building inspector never batted an eye as he made red checks on the inspection report resting on his protruding belly. He signed it, tore off the top copy and handed it to Hannah. "Good luck with this, young lady. I sure was looking forward to tasting a lobster roll but I don't see that happening for a while. Caroline always did them up with flair. No offense or anything," he finally gave Hannah a once over from the long braid hanging over her right shoulder to her flip-flop-clad feet, "but you don't look old enough to fill her shoes."

Hannah held the paper in front of her face but all she saw was red. Red check marks mocking her like nasty little wasp stings. Why did everyone think she wouldn't be able to manage the business her Great Aunt Caroline willed to her only a few months ago? A snack bar and four cottages on the beach. She'd show them all!

"Don't worry, I'll get right on these problems." Cal Murphy, the local contractor and Hannah's handyman from the day she inherited her ocean paradise, added, "I'll work all night if that's what it takes."

Hannah's grumpy elderly neighbor, Jack, scratched his head. "You'll definitely be putting in some overtime. You guys really dropped the ball this time. Didn't I tell you to check those beams? Caroline neglected maintenance on this place for years." Jack shrugged and peeked over Hannah's shoulder at the report. "There's a lot of red on that sheet."

Right, Hannah thought. All Jack was good for lately was pointing out the obvious and pointing blame at her or Cal. And making the most delicious coffee she'd ever had. That was something, she grudgingly admitted to herself.

Cal hustled off to his truck to get the needed supplies.

Meg, who had become Hannah's right hand helper and sometime surrogate mother figure, draped her arm around Hannah's shoulder. "Got a minute? There's a problem in Cottage Two."

"Can it wait?" Jack asked. "Hannah has a lot on her plate at the moment."

"I just saw the inspector leave. Is the snack bar good to go?" Meg looked from Jack's face to Hannah's. "Oh. I guess there's a problem. Want me to call my brother? He's had lots of experience with permits and all that red tape rigmarole. They're always trying to shut down his Pub and Pool Hall." She grinned. "And the inspector hasn't had any luck yet!"

"Yes, give him a call. Let me know what advice he has." She turned to Jack. "Can you keep an eye on the office? The first guests are supposed to be arriving any minute."

Jack walked toward the office, mumbling, "I'll make a fresh pot of coffee. Everything'll look better after a dose of caffeine."

As soon as Meg finished her call, she caught up with Hannah at the door of Cottage Two. "A pipe burst in the bathroom but I have the main water shut off until Cal can fix it."

"Great," Hannah mumbled. "Cal's gone to get supplies to fix the rotten beams under the snack bar. Who's supposed to be staying here?"

Meg checked the notes on her phone. "Someone named Lenny DiMarco, but he's not arriving until late afternoon."

"Call your brother again and ask him to recommend a plumber. I don't want to take Cal away from working on the snack bar. Are Cottage Three and Four all set?"

Meg had her phone out. "As far as I can tell, but better take another look just in case I missed anything. The honeymoon couple, Aaron and Laura Masterson, will be in Cottage Four so I added some special touches—a bud vase with roses, and chocolates on the pillows. Hope that's okay?"

"Yeah, yeah. Good idea. How about Cottage Three?"

Meg consulted her notes again. "A retired teacher, Sherry Wolfe. She's hoping to get to know the area and may relocate to Hooks Harbor. I'm guessing she's going to be a royal pain in the neck. I saw plenty of that type when I was working for your Great Aunt Caroline; always sticking their nose in everyone's business. They expect the perfect paradise but, of course, with the first little thing that goes wrong they moan and complain the loudest."

"At least we're booked," Hannah said distractedly as she headed away from Meg on her way to Cottage Four. Her mind was stuck on the inspector's report. Great Aunt Caroline's money was dwindling quickly with the extra repairs that kept popping up.

If she didn't get the snack bar open and keep the cottages full every day . . . well, that just wasn't an option.

Hannah was more determined than ever to prove that she could turn this inheritance into a profitable business. Especially since she was only twenty seven with no experience running anything except a dog walking service that lasted for about a month when she was living in California. Her own sister Ruby managed to be lukewarm and less than helpful when it came to helping Hannah. She ran off to who knows where right at the last minute when Hannah needed an extra pair of hands. And, Ruby left her five year old daughter, Olivia, with Hannah.

Hannah shook her head. Enough of the pity party, she told herself as she entered Cottage Four. She needed to get everything squared away before the bus dropped Olivia off at three thirty in case Ruby wasn't back when she promised.

Everything in the cozy room looked bright and cheerful. The gauzy curtains filtered the strong sunshine flooding in. Hannah pushed the bathroom door open and the faint scent of lavender soap hit her nose. That was another good suggestion from Meg, she noted. Just to be on the safe side, Hannah turned on all the faucets and flushed the toilet. Everything was in working order, thank goodness.

She brushed a few stray hairs away from her face and returned to the porch at the front of the cottage. Hannah gazed at the ocean. This cottage had the best view in her opinion. It was farthest from the beach, but also more secluded, which she thought was perfect for the honeymooners.

A young couple approached her. They leaned into each other as the young woman whispered in her partner's ear. They both giggled. Hannah imagined what secret they might be sharing and she felt her checks get hot. Yes, it was a perfect spot for romance.

Jack's body tilted to his right with their suitcase almost dragging in the sand as he struggled to keep up with the couple. His face was a neutral mask but Hannah knew he was beyond frustrated and kept his anger hidden.

"Welcome to Holiday Hideaway." Hannah extended her hand to the young couple.

Jack dropped the suitcase on the porch. "Hannah, this is Aaron and Laura Masterson. Aaron and Laura, this is Hannah, owner of Holiday Hideaway and Snack Bar."

"Hannah? I heard the owner was an old lady named Caroline?"

"That was my great aunt. She left this business to me. I've spent the last several months updating everything. I hope you enjoy your stay." Hannah stepped around the couple who acted eager to get inside.

Jack leaned close to Hannah as they walked back along the path. "You made the right choice to keep them as far away from the other guests as possible. They can't keep their hands off each other."

Hannah chuckled. "Wishing you were about sixty years younger, Jack?"

Jack's eyebrows rose. "Me? Heck no. I think a quiet lady who wants to sit and watch the sunset with me would be nice though. And if she drives a red sports car that would be a plus."

Hannah put her arm around her friend. "You never know, Jack. You never know."

Jack finally rewarded Hannah with a small smile.

As they reached the office attached to Cottage One, where Hannah lived, a middle aged woman was waiting for them. She brushed some dust from her dark blue sweatpants before launching into her banter. "This is such a fabulous spot. I'm thrilled to find it. Am I early? Can I get into my room? My feet are killing me."

Hannah's eyes glanced sideways at Jack. "Um, have a seat." She extended her hand. "Sherry Wolfe?"

The woman nodded and opened her mouth to jabber some more but Hannah cut her off.

"I'll get you checked in."

"I'm starving. I hope I can get something at that cute snack bar. Maybe a bowl of clam chowder to take to my cottage?"

Hannah blinked. Apparently Mrs. Wolfe only had one speed with her talking. "Unfortunately, the snack bar won't open until Saturday." Hannah crossed her fingers that that didn't turn into a lie.

"Oh dear, you'll have to point me in the right direction to get a bite to eat in town. Nothing big, mind you." She patted her stomach. "Just a snack to tide me over until dinner."

"Of course. There's a brochure in your cottage with a list of all the local spots with directions and phone numbers. I'm sure you'll be able to find something suitable. Now, let me grab the key and Jack will get you settled into Cottage Three."

Jack mumbled something slightly insulting under his breath that was completely lost on Mrs. Wolfe. Hannah handed the key to Jack. He looked miserable. Hannah tried to keep the corners of her lips from twitching up into a laugh until they were out of the office. Mrs. Wolfe's dialogue never stopped until Jack let her into the cottage. For all Hannah knew, it didn't stop then, either, but at least she couldn't hear it.

Before Hannah had a chance to catch her breath after Sherry's whirlwind entrance, Meg arrived in the office with the plumber her brother sent over. "Want me to show Bill the problem?"

"Thanks, Meg. You're a lifesaver."

Jack waited quietly until Meg left. "You owe me big time, Hannah Holiday. That woman doesn't even stop to breathe! She asked me on a date! Can you believe it?"

Hannah peeked at the cars in the parking lot. "Too bad she's not driving a red sports car or maybe you would have been tempted," Hannah said between chuckles.

"No. I said someone *quiet* to watch the sunset with me. Not a motormouth."

"Shhh. Here she comes."

Mrs. Wolfe wiggled her fingers as she walked to her car. "Toodle-oo Jack. See you later."

"I doubt it," Hannah heard him mumble under his breath. "I'm going home for a rest."

Hannah sat at her desk to sort through a pile of invoices. She quickly added up the amounts and saw her bank balance shrink to an uncomfortable low.

"Knock knock," a husky voice broke through her concentration.

"Can I help you?" Hannah looked up into an extremely tanned, rugged face. His eyes perfectly matched the blue of his t-shirt and his smile told Annie he knew women found him irresistible.

"I'm Lenny DiMarco. Holiday Hideaway, right? I have a reservation for today?"

Hannah stood up. "Of course. I wasn't expecting you until late afternoon. Your cottage isn't quite ready."

"No problem. If I could just drop off my things? I'm heading to the Bayside Marina for an hour or two. I want to explore the coastline. Maybe check out some good fishing spots."

Hannah couldn't help but notice how handsome Lenny was—tall and muscular with curly hair and that two day unshaven casual style. Not that Hannah was in the market for a boyfriend, but maybe Ruby?

He smiled. "Will that be okay?"

Hannah felt heat rise to her cheeks realizing that Lenny noticed her staring at him. "Sure. I'll show you where your cottage is." She stood up too quickly and her chair tipped over backwards.

Lenny grinned but said nothing.

Hannah grabbed the key. "This way." She felt his eyes on her backside all the way to Cottage Two.

She stopped to let Lenny enter. He squinted his eyes as he studied her face. "You look familiar. Have we met before?"

"No, I don't think so." Another rush of heat went straight to her cheeks even though she decided that was probably his standard pick-up line. "Okay then. Everything should be ready by the time you return."

"Great. I'm really excited. I've got a boat rented and waiting for me." Lenny dropped his bags inside, smiled at Hannah, and headed back to his truck.

Hannah was pleased to see Cal working on the snack bar. She had confidence he would fix all the problems so she'd be able to open on Saturday.

Cal slid his hammer into his tool belt and leaned against the building. "Who's the new guy?" he asked with a hint of disapproval.

"One of the guests. He's off to rent a boat to check out the coastline."

"Hope he's familiar with the rocky outcrops. They've gotten many experienced boaters in trouble." Cal nodded toward the plumber's truck. "What's Bill doing here?"

"A broken water line in Cottage Two. I didn't want to take you away from this problem." She pointed to the snack bar.

"I've got it all figured out. I should be finished with all the problems on the inspection sheet by tomorrow. Is Meg ready to get rolling with the cooking?"

"Boy, I hope so. I'm counting on her. I'm not sure I can handle it if anything else goes wrong."

The squeal of the school bus brakes interrupted their conversation. "Three thirty all ready?" Hannah said. "Ruby should be getting back soon, too. She promised she'd only be gone for two nights. I love having Olivia here but it's so much harder to get anything done."

Olivia skipped toward Cal and Hannah with her giant pink backpack slapping against her back. Nellie, Hannah's overgrown one year old golden retriever, woke from her nap and charged over to greet Olivia. Olivia screeched with joy as Nellie licked her face.

"Good thing Ruby isn't here to see that or she'd be washing poor Olivia's face with wipes. She blames dog germs every time Olivia gets sick." Hannah crouched down to hug the kindergartner.

"Is mommy home yet?"

Hannah scanned the road. "Close your eyes and count to ten, then she'll be here."

Olivia dutifully counted with her hands covering her eyes. She only made it to five before she stopped and yelled, "Mommy!"

"I think she peeked," Cal said as he chuckled at his biggest little fan.

Ruby lifted Olivia and twirled her in a circle. "Let's thank Aunt Hannah before we head home. I have a surprise for you when I unpack."

The small talk didn't take long since Olivia wanted to go home and get her surprise. Cal returned to his project of removing the rotten beams under the snack bar and Hannah walked back toward her office. She was surprised to see the young honeymoon couple rushing toward her, their faces pale and drawn with panic.

Aaron had his arms raised and he waved them wildly. As he got closer to Hannah, he rested his hands on his knees and gasped out the message, "Call the police. There's a capsized boat up the beach."

Hannah's blood ran cold. Could it be Lenny?

Chapter 2

Reacting on a surge of adrenaline, Hannah told Aaron to wait in Cottage Four.

Without thinking it through, Hannah sprinted to Cottage Two. Who was this guy Lenny DiMarco? She called the police station. Her curiosity soared and her feet took her into Lenny's cottage. Her fingers hovered over his bags. This was so wrong, she told herself, but if he was in trouble, maybe knowing more about him could help the police. She had time to take a quick look in his bags before anyone arrived. No one would know.

Hannah ignored the big duffel bag and opened a smaller camera bag, hoping she might find a clue if he had left his camera behind. A beautiful professional looking Nikon camera sat nestled inside the bag.

Her fingers hesitated before snatching up the camera and hitting the power button. What if Lenny returned, she thought. This was completely inappropriate. She stood up and looked toward the driveway. No one in sight.

Hannah scrolled through the digital images and froze. What met her eyes made absolutely no sense. Why did Lenny have images of Ruby on his camera? Was he stalking her?

She quickly returned the camera to its case, her fingers fumbling with the zipper. She slung the bag over her shoulder and hustled to her office. She stashed the bag under the big desk that once belonged to her Great Aunt Caroline. Hannah wondered what other secrets that old scarred desk hid over the years.

The sound of sirens got louder and louder. Hannah's body trembled. What if she stole evidence, *or* what if it wasn't Lenny's capsized boat and he returned to find his camera bag missing? She called Ruby.

Without a hello, Hannah said, "Get over her quick. Without Olivia."

"What's going on?" Ruby asked.

"Just hurry." Hannah disconnected the call as she saw Officer Pam Larson walking toward the office escorted by Cal.

She inhaled a deep calming breath and let it out slowly before Pam pulled the door open.

Pam stood with her hands on her hips. "What mess did you fall into now?" she sneered.

Jack barged in behind Pam and Cal. "I heard the siren. What happened?"

Pam looked at her father. "I don't know yet. She," Pam waved her hand at Hannah, "called in a report of a capsized boat. The chief is out investigating now. I got sent here to question Ms. Holiday."

Hannah needed fresh air. With everyone crowded into her small office, she suddenly felt light headed. "My guests, Aaron and Laura Masterson, told me to call the police. They saw the capsized boat." She moved toward the door, hoping everyone would get the message and exit.

"Where are they?" Pam asked.

"I told them to wait in Cottage Four."

Miraculously, Jack, Cal, and Pam walked outside. Hannah followed, letting the fresh air revive her.

"Are you all right?" Cal held Hannah's arm. "You look like you're about to faint."

She waved her hand in front of her face. "I'm better. The fresh air is helping."

Cal and Hannah lingered behind the others as Jack led his daughter to Cottage Four. Cal asked quietly. "What's going on? A capsized boat isn't so unusual."

"I'm not sure. I need to talk to Ruby about something I found." Hannah hesitated. "Something that Lenny left here."

Cal's eyes widened. "Lenny? The guy renting a boat?"

"Yeah. Didn't you say the area he was going to could be treacherous?"

"I did. But lots of people are out on the water. What's the chance it's *his* boat? That's what you're thinking, right?"

She nodded. They were close enough to hear Pam talking to Aaron about what he saw and where they were walking.

Pam's radio blasted a message. "Capsized boat found and identified. Rented by a Lenny DiMarco."

Hannah gripped Cal's arm. "I have to go back and wait for Ruby."

"Wait a minute, Ms. Holiday." Pam's icy voice stopped Hannah in her tracks. "Dad just told me Lenny DiMarco was registered to stay here. Did he ever arrive?"

"Ah, yeah, he did, but his cottage wasn't ready so he dropped off a bag and left. He said he would be back later." Her hands were shaking. She knew she was hiding what could be evidence under her desk.

"Where's the bag?"

"Cottage Two."

"Did anyone look at it?"

"No." Hannah felt sweat drip down her side. That wasn't a lie. No one went through *that* bag. She would be in a boatload of trouble if Pam discovered Hannah was hiding the camera bag. Too late to worry about that now.

"Get me the bag. Meet me in your office." Pam didn't mince words, or her attitude. Hannah went to retrieve Lenny's bag. Something about the way he had looked at her earlier made her skin crawl. Had he been stalking her *and* Ruby? Why?

Cal jogged to keep up. "You're hiding something. It's written all over your face. You better pull yourself together before Pam gets to your office."

Hannah stopped and turned on Cal. "If you want to help, head Ruby off before she walks into my office. Send her to Jack's house to wait."

Cal said nothing but headed to the road.

"Cal?"

He stopped and turned around.

"Thank you, Cal. I can't tell you more because I don't know what's going on, but I'm afraid Ruby might be in trouble."

He nodded and picked up his pace just as Ruby's car drove into sight.

Hannah picked up Lenny's bag, surprised at how light it was, and carried it to her office. Her curiosity was killing her to open the bag and look inside but she resisted. Instead, she opened a bottle of water and chugged half of it. She certainly didn't need her mouth to go dry while she was being grilled by Pam.

Footsteps stomped up the office porch steps. "The bag?" Pam said as she pointed to Lenny's duffle on Hannah's desk.

"Yes."

"If he shows up, tell him I've got it at the police station."

"And if he doesn't?" Hannah asked.

Pam turned back to face Hannah with her head cocked to one side. "What is it to you?"

Hannah shrugged and forced herself to keep her mouth shut. She didn't want to ratchet up any higher on Pam's radar.

"I suppose if we find a body, you might have to identify him. Who else in town knows this guy?"

"Maybe Chase Fuller from the marina. Lenny told me he was renting a boat there."

"That's helpful. I'll go find out what Chase knows."

Pam left. With the duffle and no thank you.

Jack eyed Hannah. "Where's Cal? He scurried off like he was on a mission. And you look like you swallowed a canary. I doubt Pam missed that look on your face. What are you not telling her?"

"You don't want to know, Jack. Pam's your daughter. And a police officer. Besides, it might be nothing."

Ruby pushed the door open and entered with Cal right behind. "What's going on? You tell me to hurry, then Cal sends me to hide out at Jack's house. Have you gone mad, Hannah?"

Jack and Cal sat down. Should she ask them to leave? They'd always had her back in the past.

Three sets of eyes bored into her. Waiting for an explanation. Hannah pulled the camera bag from its hiding spot. She placed it on the desk and unzipped the bag.

Ruby stroked her chin and raised her eyes to Hannah's.

"Do you know a guy named Lenny DiMarco?" Hannah asked, her voice deathly quiet.

Ruby barely nodded her head yes.

"You've seen this camera before?"

Again she nodded and whispered. "Why do you have it?"

"We probably shouldn't have this conversation here."

Jack stood up. "I'll make coffee at my house. Cal can keep an eye on the office and call you if another problem pops up."

"Another problem?" Hannah said with raised eyebrows. She laughed because if she didn't, she'd probably cry. She pulled her long braid and chewed on the end. She had three days to get her snack bar through the building inspection or she'd miss her grand opening. A water line burst in one of the cottages. At least, as far as she knew, that problem was taken care of. And now, Ruby had some explaining to do. Nothing else could go wrong, right?

Cal reluctantly said he'd get back to the repairs on the snack bar and watch the office. Hannah didn't stop him.

Finally, she was alone with Ruby. "Who is Lenny DiMarco? How do you know him?"

Ruby slumped into a chair. "I can't tell you."

Hannah sat down and zipped the camera bag closed. "Okay. I'll just hand this over to Officer Larson along with the duffle bag she already confiscated."

Ruby jumped up. "Why is that bag even here? Or his duffle bag?" Her fingers combed through her short brown hair. "Was he renting one of the cottages?"

"He was. I'm not sure if he'll be back or not since the boat he rented was found capsized."

"And Lenny?" Ruby asked, her eyes wide.

Hannah shrugged. "I don't know. But let's get back to this camera. I looked through some of the images."

Ruby's face fell into her hands. "Don't tell me what you found. How bad is it?"

Hannah stood up and walked around her desk. She crouched in front of Ruby. "I have no idea how bad it is. The first question should be—why are there photos of you on his camera? I took the bag on impulse when I heard a boat had capsized. I'm in trouble whether he comes back or not. If Pam finds out, she'll hound me out of town for tampering with evidence, and if Lenny comes back he could give me some pretty bad publicity for stealing his stuff. Now, did I expose myself to those kinds of problems, to protect you I might add, for nothing?"

"Lenny is Olivia's dad." Ruby mumbled. "He doesn't know. He can't find out."

Hannah shook Ruby's shoulders. "What did you say?"

"I left for the past two days to try to appease him. He was holed up in someone's house about ten miles from here and he said if I didn't go visit, he'd come find me." Ruby finally looked at Hannah. "Find me and Olivia."

"Lenny? That's the guy you've been running and hiding from these last five years since Olivia was born? Why? He's gorgeous. When I saw him it even crossed my mind that he was just your type."

"Yeah, well, looks are deceiving. Turns out he's a slimy operator who will do anything for a buck. And I mean anything. I had to protect Olivia. What was he doing renting a boat?"

Hannah sat back in her chair. "Lenny didn't give me his detailed itinerary. All he said was he planned to explore the coastline. Any idea what he was looking for?"

Ruby unzipped the camera bag. "I bet there's a clue here." She searched through the images and stopped to show one to Hannah. "Here's an image of a map. Once, he mentioned a treasure map that would make him rich. I assumed it was just more of his grandiose schemes, but maybe he was after some kind of treasure. Does this map make any sense to you?"

Hannah studied the image. "Not really, but the shoreline isn't my specialty. Cal or Jack might recognize something."

"We can't tell them about Lenny. No one can know Olivia is his child."

"What else aren't you telling me, Ruby?"

Ruby's face went pale and her foot jiggled until her shoe flopped off. "Let's get some of Jack's coffee before it's cold."

They left the office and walked slowly toward Jack's house.

Ruby broke the silence and her words couldn't have shocked Hannah more. "Lenny has connections to the mob."

Chapter 3

Wednesday ended. Finally. When Hannah opened her eyes Thursday morning, she considered closing them and staying in bed. But it was a new day, she felt refreshed, and Nellie whined to go outside. Blue sky again. The peaceful sound of waves crashed on the beach and a salty breeze blew through the partly opened window. Today had to be filled with less drama. Right?

Wrong!

Hannah couldn't believe her eyes.

A red Mazda Miata convertible screeched to a halt in front of her snack bar.

Hannah blinked. Was she awake or dreaming? Or had her mind finally crashed over the deep end?

A miniature pig, wearing pink sunglasses and a sunhat, sat in the passenger seat of the convertible.

Hannah closed her eyes and shook her head. After counting to ten, she opened them, expecting blue sky and the peaceful ocean view to be all that met her eyes.

No such luck.

A voice hollered from the driver's seat. "Am I on time?"

"Excuse me?" Hannah asked.

"Am I on time? I got a letter from Caroline Holiday inviting me to meet the new owner of her cottages." The woman removed her scarf to reveal purple streaked silver hair, neatly curled but slightly flattened. She said something to her passenger before she opened the car door and climbed out. The passenger responded with a snort.

As Hannah watched the unfolding scene, she realized her mouth was hanging open. Who was this person and what was up with the pig? And the biggest question of all was—when did Great Aunt Caroline send a letter to this person? Hannah didn't know she would inherit the ocean-side property on the coast of Maine until the lawyer called her after Caroline died last year. Did

Caroline have all this planned before she died?

"Hello," the woman said, waving her hand in front of Hannah's face. "Where's Caroline?"

"Why is there a pig in your car?"

The woman's hands flew up. "Oh. Of course. Petunia needs to get out. We've been driving all night." She opened the passenger door and the small pig hopped out and started to root around in the sand.

Nellie sniffed the pig and wagged her tail. She got down on her two front paws in a play bow and the pig charged. Hannah was speechless. The woman screeched with delight and the pig chased Nellie.

The woman brought her attention back to Hannah. "It looks like Petunia found a friend. I'm guessing Caroline isn't here at the moment? Where should I put my stuff?"

Hannah watched as Jack walked around the convertible and carefully wiped a speck of dirt off the hood. "Did you trade in your old Volvo for this beauty, Hannah?"

Hannah shook her head and nodded toward the purple haired old lady standing next to her.

"Jack? Is that you? Haven't seen you in a million years! Remember when you, me, and Caroline went skinny dipping and shocked all her guests?"

"Pearl Amato?"

Pearl flicked her wrist. "Pearl Martini now. Tony Amato and I split up thirty years ago. The only plus from that marriage is Rocky." She eyed Hannah. "He's about your age, honey. Are you looking for a man?"

"You have a son *my* age?" Hannah asked with her eyes opened wide.

"Oh no, honey. He's my grandson."

Jack saved Hannah. "What in tarnation are you doing here, Pearl? Caroline's going to be mighty pissed that you didn't come before she kicked the bucket."

The color under Pearl's heavily powdered face drained away. "Dead? Caroline is dead? When? Why didn't anyone tell me?" She held up a letter. "I got this from her just a couple of weeks ago."

Jack snatched the letter from Pearl's hand. "That doesn't make sense. It must have gotten lost in the mail somewhere. Caroline died last year." He studied the letter and read out loud, "*Pearl, come meet the new owner of my cottages. You can stay for as long as you like.*" Jack looked up. "Something doesn't add up. It was postmarked on March twelfth of this year—that's a year after she died. Exactly."

Before they could come up with any more speculation about Great Aunt Caroline, Sherry Wolfe screamed and jumped behind Jack. She wrapped her arms around his waist and held on tight. "What's that pig doing? Is it going to hurt me?"

"Hurt you?" Pearl huffed in a most grumpy tone. "Your screaming probably scarred her for life. And let go of Jack. You aren't his type." Pearl crouched down.

"Come to mommy my wittle snufflebug." She dug around in her skirt pocket and extracted a handful of grapes that Petunia gobbled from her hand.

Pearl hooked a leash onto Petunia's harness and stood up. "So, which cottage are we staying in?"

Sherry pointed at Petunia. "If that swine stays here, I'm leaving."

"Don't slam the door on your way out," Pearl said and headed to the office. "I'll wait in there for someone to help me."

Sherry glared at Hannah. "Well?"

Hannah's head was spinning. This day started with more drama than she wanted in a whole month. "I'm sorry Mrs. Wolfe. This, um, visitor dropped in unexpectedly, but since she was invited by my Great Aunt Caroline who left this beautiful business to me, I feel I have to honor the invitation. But don't worry, I will insist that Petunia doesn't bother you." What she left unsaid was that she wouldn't be surprised if a *ton* of bother followed Pearl and Petunia to her beautiful ocean cottages.

"Well, I'll trust you to keep a tight ship here," she complained as she checked her watch. "I'll have to walk double time to keep on my schedule."

Jack and Hannah watched Sherry's receding figure walk at a brisk pace, her backpack reflecting the morning sun.

Hannah jabbed Jack in the side. "What were you telling me about a red convertible yesterday? Maybe you and Pearl? Meant to be?"

"I don't think so. She's a wild one, a friend of Caroline's from waaaay back. I only met her the one time we went skinny dipping, but Caroline shared a lot more stories that will never pass these lips." He moved his fingers as if zipping his mouth closed.

"Maybe she's changed," Hannah said with one eyebrow up.

"Maybe *not*. Did you look at her? Purple hair, purple eye shadow, a hippy dippy skirt, *and* a pig? She's more woman than I can manage. Everything screams loud and obnoxious." Jack lowered his voice. "Caroline told me Pearl's first husband, Tony Amato, had ties to the mob. Can you imagine what Pam would say about that?"

Hannah laughed. "Okay. You've made your point. Thanks for the background info. I'll see if I can get her to stay at the Paradise Inn instead of here. I'm booked. There are no empty cottages."

"Not technically," Jack stated. "But Cottage Two looks pretty empty to me. What do you think happened to that Lenny guy? If he's the one in that capsized boat, you'll have an empty cottage for Pearl."

Cal's truck drove in loaded with new beams for the snack bar. "Looks like I'm late for the party. Whose flashy convertible is this?"

"Don't ask," Jack said.

"You'll meet her soon enough I'm sure," Hannah added.

"Her?" Cal asked with too much enthusiasm.

Hannah smacked his arm. "Yeah, *her*, but she's a bit too old for you. Jack skinny dipped with her and Caroline many moons ago."

Cal wiggled his eyebrows and elbowed Jack. "Sounds like a catch."

"I'm going home for breakfast. I'll be back in a while," Jack said, ignoring Cal's dig.

"Is she that bad?" Cal asked

"I'll let you judge for yourself. But watch out for her pig, Petunia."

"What?"

Hannah laughed at Cal's confused expression and walked to her office, hoping to have some luck sorting out her new weird problem.

The first thing Hannah noticed when she opened her office door was the smell of cigarette smoke. The second thing was the sound of Pearl sobbing. Hannah waved her hand in front of her face and coughed. "Sorry, but there's no smoking in here."

Pearl stabbed her cigarette out in an empty coffee mug. She hastily wiped her cheeks. "I gave up smoking ages ago but I keep one for emergencies. Hearing the news about poor Caroline made me remember how we used to sneak out of her bedroom window when we were kids to smoke on the roof. That cigarette was for her, wherever she may be." Pearl made a grand gesture upward with her arms.

"About accommodations," Hannah began.

Pearl stroked Petunia. Hannah couldn't be sure, but it sounded like Petunia was purring, or maybe it was soft grunting. Whatever it was, she was beginning to think Petunia was adorable.

"Don't worry. We don't need anything fancy. You can put us anywhere." Pearl dabbed her eyes carefully, just enough to absorb the tears but not smudge the purple eye shadow. "And there's something else."

Hannah sat down opposite Pearl and Petunia. She waited as patiently as possible.

Pearl sighed. "Now that I'm getting over my initial shock and I have a good look at you, I should have realized from the moment I saw you that you must be Caroline's great niece, Hannah. The new owner."

Hannah nodded.

"You are the spitting image of Caroline." She cocked her head sideways. "It's a bit eerie, to be truthful." She smoothed a piece of paper on the desk and slid it toward Hannah. "Take a look at this. It came with the letter."

Hannah picked up the paper. It was a crudely drawn map. She'd seen something like it right after she moved in. A treasure map that Jack was keeping safe and sound as far as she knew.

Pearl continued. "To tell you the truth, the map is what really intrigued me. Caroline and I had a falling out years ago so I was actually a bit worried about seeing her again." Pearl placed Petunia on the floor and she stood up. "Where am I staying?"

For some reason Hannah couldn't turn Pearl away. Was it the connection to Caroline and the possibility to find out more about her great aunt? Or was it the treasure map? Or was it Pearl's quirkiness and Petunia's endearing cuteness? Whatever it was, Hannah didn't have time to do any deep analysis. Instead she said, "Follow me."

Hannah led Pearl and Petunia to Cottage Two. She had no idea what she would do if Lenny showed up but she'd cross that problem when she had to. Plus the issue of his camera bag. She unlocked the door, holding it open for her guests to enter. "You can stay here for as long as you like."

"I don't expect I'll stay for longer than a week. Petunia and I have reservations for a cruise."

The door closed just as Hannah heard Cal call her name. As she turned, her flip flop skidded on the sandy wood and she found herself sprawled at the bottom of the deck steps. Her knees and the palms of her hands burned from the slide. She groaned. Bad karma for letting Pearl stay in Lenny's cottage?

"Hannah, what happened?" Cal crouched down in front of her.

She kicked off her flip flops and dusted the sand off her hands as best she could. "I slipped." She pushed herself to her knees and Cal helped her to her feet. "You called me. What's the problem now?" She heard the annoyance in her voice and felt bad to take it out on Cal. He was only trying to help.

"I just heard that a body has been sighted," he answered as they walked toward the office.

She froze. "I have to go into town to find out more."

Chapter 4

Hannah drove straight to Ruby's house in town. She pulled up in time to join Ruby as she walked Olivia to school. The short walk and Olivia's calming chatter gave Hannah time to sort her thoughts and make a plan. Olivia hugged her mom and aunt before running off to her kindergarten line.

"I wasn't expecting to see you this early, don't you have a million things to take care of before your snack bar opens on Saturday?" Ruby asked as they walked side by side.

"This visit wasn't on my agenda until about twenty minutes ago when Cal informed me that a body was sighted. We need to find out if it's Lenny. He never returned to his cottage so my guess is he won't be bothering you anymore."

Ruby opened her front door. Hannah inhaled the scent of coffee. "Have anything to go with that coffee?"

"Blueberry muffins? How does that sound?"

"Perfect." Hannah found two mugs and poured coffee while Ruby put the muffins on a plate. They sat opposite each other at the small round table in Ruby's kitchen.

"Here's what I'm thinking," Hannah said. "We'll head over to the Bayside Marina and find out what Chase Fuller knows. He rented the boat to Lenny that capsized, so with some luck, he may be able to fill us in with some details we don't already know. I can use the excuse that Lenny was renting a cottage from me and I'm concerned about his whereabouts, blah, blah, blah. Chase likes to talk about himself so you can stroke his ego about how great his Bayside Marina looks or what a flattering haircut he has or whatever you think of. Just figure out how to flatter him so he wants to share information with us."

"So if the body is Lenny, we wipe our hands and walk away like we know nothing about him?" Ruby asked.

"Exactly."

"And if the body *isn't* Lenny?" Ruby asked with a fearful look in her eyes.

"Who else could it be? Was anyone else at that house when you visited him?"

"I didn't see anyone, but if I know anything about Lenny, he always had an escape plan." Ruby chewed on her lower lip and absentmindedly picked blueberries out of her muffin.

"You think he planned this accident to fake his own death?"

"Listen Hannah. I don't know what to think, all right? I've been running away from this man for over five years and he always manages to pop back into the edge of my life like a bad nightmare. Until I see the body, I refuse to assume he's dead."

Hannah nodded her head. "Fair enough. I'll add *see the body* to our plan." She wrote an imaginary note on an invisible piece of paper.

"Another thing that has been bothering me," Ruby paused and waited for Hannah's full attention, "why did he show up to rent one of *your* cottages and leave his bags behind? Do you think he could have connected us and now he'll use you to get to me?"

Hannah waved her hand dismissively. "Of course, that would assume he's still alive. I'm sure it's just a coincidence." Or was it, she wondered. The remark Lenny made to Hannah about whether they met before and how he studied her face now had new meaning. Anyone would know in the blink of an eye that Ruby and Hannah were sisters. He knew. It must be part of his game plan. Hannah decided not to alarm Ruby with that detail. Yet.

Hannah finished her coffee and last bite of muffin before she pushed her chair back. "Let's get going. I do need to get back to my cottages before Sherry Wolfe runs into Petunia again. With my luck, Petunia will root around in Sherry's backpack and eat her snacks."

Ruby gave Hannah a puzzled look. "Who is Petunia?"

"Actually, she's a pot belly pig that arrived this morning with an interesting, to put it mildly, old friend of Great Aunt Caroline's. You'll have to bring Olivia around after school. She'll *love* Petunia."

They walked to the marina with the sound of helicopters overhead. "I thought you said they found a body," Ruby said.

"Yeah. That's what I heard." They continued in silence, Hannah worrying more and more that *if* a body was found and *if* they were still searching, it could only mean one thing—the body wasn't that of Lenny DiMarco.

Hannah was startled from her daydream when Sherry Wolfe called to her. "Hannah? Is that you?" Sherry picked up her pace to catch up with Hannah and Ruby. "What's going on here? I was walking on the beach and the peace and quiet was completely destroyed by the horrible helicopter flying overhead and boats patrolling the shoreline."

"There's been an accident, Sherry. I don't know the particulars yet."

Sherry's hand went to her mouth. "Oh dear. A boating accident?"

"Yes. That's what it sounds like."

"Oh dear," she said again. "This vacation is not turning out to be the relaxing getaway I was so hoping for. That pig almost gave me a heart attack, and now this." She pulled a packet of crackers from her pocket and stuffed one in her mouth. "I hope things get back to normal. What is normal for this town?" she asked with bits of cracker spraying from her mouth.

Hannah smiled, hoping to distract Sherry. "This is a wonderful town with lots of interesting activities. Since you like walking, you might want to join the birder group on Saturday or go to the open house at Simply Sweets and sample their new chocolate creations."

"Oh, chocolate, now you've hit my weak spot. Thanks for the tips. Toodle-oo."

"One of your guests?" Ruby asked after Sherry was out of earshot.

"Yup. Kind of needy, I think she'll be a handful."

They turned into the driveway for the Bayside Marina, and by the looks of the parking lot, it had been transformed into rescue central. The parking area was cleared of cars for a landing space for the helicopter. Hannah saw the back of Officer Pam Larson and, over her shoulder, Chase Fuller's scowling face. He was getting a grilling which wouldn't put him in an agreeable mood. Hopefully Ruby was on her best charm and flatter A-game if they had any hope of pumping Chase for information about Lenny.

Pam marched off when the helicopter landed. Fortunately, she never saw Hannah and Ruby.

Hannah called to Chase. He hesitated, then walked toward the two women. "I'm busy, and this disaster is hurting my business. What do you want?"

Hannah started in, "I know exactly how you feel, Chase. Lenny was staying in one of my cottages and I'm trying to find out what happened to him."

Ruby moved closer to Chase. "You're marina is much too popular for this to have any lasting repercussions." She fluttered her lashes shamelessly.

"Well," Chase's shoulders relaxed. He looked around and hustled them to a far corner away from the police milling about. "I don't know much but I'll share this— Lenny DiMarco came across as an arrogant know-it-all, and if he got into trouble on the rocky point where the boat capsized, he's got no one to blame but himself. I tried to warn him to stay away from that area, especially at high tide. The unfortunate thing is," Chase lowered his voice, "the body they found isn't Lenny."

Ruby's fingers tightened on Hannah's arm. "Who was it?" she asked.

"I can't figure it out. I never saw anyone get in the boat with him. That's what Officer Larson was interrogating me about. She thinks I'm hiding something to help Lenny."

"Why would she think that?"

Chase shrugged. "Because I rented the boat to him? I don't know. I never met the guy before."

"Thanks for the information, Chase. One more question—did they identify the dead guy yet?"

"If they did, they aren't sharing the information." He waved his arm up in the air. "And as you can see, they're still searching for Lenny. No one thinks he could survive the cold water or the rocks. He may never be found if he got battered to bits."

"Wouldn't *something* float ashore?"

"It's possible. Maybe some clothing. He could even be wedged in an underwater crevice. At any rate, I don't think you should expect him back at your cottage, Hannah." Chase walked through the police to his office and slammed the door.

"Let's get out of here, Ruby. I don't want Officer Larson to spot us." Hannah pulled Ruby's arm to get her moving.

Ruby didn't budge. "Lenny's not dead. I know it," she mumbled.

Officer Pam Larson turned around and spotted Hannah.

"Come *on* Ruby." Hannah tugged with more force.

Too late. Pam was stomping toward them.

"Don't say anything," Hannah whispered to Ruby. "Let me answer the questions."

"The Holiday sisters. What brings you to the marina? Are you planning a boating excursion?"

"Hello Pam. Just chatting with Chase. We'll be on our way now," Hannah answered as she tried to pull Ruby along with her.

"Not so fast. How did you know Lenny DiMarco, Ruby?" Pam stared at Ruby.

Just what Hannah feared. How would Ruby answer that general question? Ruby couldn't lie, but was Pam bluffing? Did she find something in Lenny's duffle bag? Hannah gave herself a good mental smack for not checking that bag, too, before Pam took it.

"Ruby?"

Ruby's mouth opened. She looked at Hannah. Hannah held her breath.

"I don't know him," Ruby lied.

"Have you ever seen him?" Pam asked.

Ruby's eyes darted between Pam and Hannah. "No," came out more like an exhaled breath of air than a word.

Pam nodded. "Let's hope he shows up safe and sound."

"What's that supposed to mean?" Hannah demanded.

"You figure it out," Pam answered as she was walking away. She stopped and turned her head back toward Hannah and Ruby. "He was a photographer. I wonder what happened to his camera."

Hannah didn't give Ruby a chance to answer. She dragged her sister back to the road and back to Ruby's house.

"Will you be okay here by yourself?" Hannah asked Ruby after she got her settled on the couch.

"I don't know. What if Lenny shows up?"

"Come home with me. Call the school and have Olivia dropped off at the cottages. She'll be happy about that change." Hannah dashed around throwing extra clothes into a bag. "Let's go. It might be time to talk to Meg's brother at the Pub and Pool Hall. He always hears what's going on around town. The juicier the better."

Hannah's phone beeped with a message from Cal. *Where r u? Got a bit of a problem here.*

Chapter 5

Hannah couldn't even pull her old Volvo station wagon into the driveway to her cottages. She parked at Jack's house. Who did all these cars belong to, she wondered as she walked to her office and Ruby vanished into Hannah's cottage.

Jack sat at Hannah's desk. "You're not going to like this. Pearl has some visitors."

"Oh?"

"Yeah, her first husband, Tony Amato, and their grandson Rocky. I don't know who the other three characters are, but I'm not sure if they have a brain between them."

"They all came in separate cars?" Hannah swiveled her head to look out the window. Five big Cadillacs were parked behind Pearl's red Mazda Miata, pulled in all willy nilly, blocking the entrance for anyone wanting to go in or out of the driveway. Great, this would give Sherry one more thing to complain about. Her little sedan wouldn't be leaving until Hannah figured out how to get rid of these people.

Cal stomped inside, obviously angry. "I can't get my truck around these boats out here, Hannah. I've got a truckload of material to unload."

Hannah put her hands up. "Okay. I'm on it." Hannah was steaming. She let Pearl finagle a cottage because of her connection to Great Aunt Caroline, but guests? This was too much. She knocked on the door of Cottage Two.

The door opened a crack. "Hey Nana. There's a cute girl out here. Can I let her in?"

Hannah's outrage flew off the chart. She stuck her foot in the door to be sure she wouldn't be locked out. She shrieked when her bare toes came in contact with something warm and wet.

The door opened a bit more. "Don't worry, Doll Face, it's just a little pig." He wiggled his eyebrows. "I'm Rocky, who are you?"

Hannah ignored the loudmouth and pushed into the room. Besides Casanova Rocky at the door, four other men either lounged on the bed or slouched on chairs watching TV. The room was filled with enough smoke to create a haze and she wondered why the smoke alarm wasn't screeching. Hannah's hands clenched into tight fists. "Who dismantled the smoke alarm? Pearl? We need to talk." Hannah stomped out to the cottage's porch and waited.

And waited.

And waited.

Petunia joined Hannah and looked up at her like she was expecting a treat. Hannah softened a bit. It wasn't Petunia's fault. She made a mental note to keep a handful of treats for Petunia in her pocket along with Nellie's dog treats.

Finally, Pearl walked through the door dressed in a long loose multi-colored muumuu and a towel wrapped around her head "Sorry. I was in the shower. Had to get the cigarette smell out of my hair."

Hannah raised her eyebrows. "The room is so filled with smoke, I almost called the fire department. Which one of your lovely guests disconnected the smoke alarm? I already have the building inspector giving me grief. Do you have any idea what he'd do if he found out about that?" Hannah clenched her jaw. "What's going on in there, Pearl? The cottage isn't big enough to accommodate all these people." What she kept to herself was that she had less than zero desire to even try to accommodate any of them, except Petunia.

"You think I want them here? My ex-husband, Tony, is inside. I can't stand him. The only reason I let him in was because Rocky's been looking out for him. They're kind of a package deal. Did you meet Rocky? My grandson, my pride and joy. He'd be *perfect* for you. You know, if you're in the market." Pearl looked hopefully at Hannah.

"I'm not, and they have to go. Now. My guests and my employees can't even get into the driveway." Hannah's voice went up with each word.

Pearl looked behind her and leaned close to Hannah. "It is starting to look like a mob convention. I'll tell them they have to leave."

"Now," Hannah reminded Pearl.

Of course Sherry would have to walk by at the moment Petunia decided to root around in front of the cottage. The smoke from Pearl's cottage was drifting outside. And, Rocky sauntered out, sans shirt. Not that he was hard to look at, but his peacock strut was enough to make Hannah gag.

Sherry's eyes popped and, without a word, she hastened to Cottage Three and slammed the door.

"What's her problem?" Rocky asked.

"A bit uptight," Pearl said. "She must need a man in her life."

"Is that your solution to every problem?" Hannah asked.

"Always worked for me, dear. Got wealthy and, I'd like to think, wise from all my ex's." Pearl winked at Hannah.

A loud crash sounded inside the cottage.

"Move the cars. All of them. Out. Of. My. Driveway. Now." Hannah kept her words level to counter her rising stress level.

"No need for attitude, Doll Face. We only stopped in to say hello to Nana," Rocky said as he grinned at Hannah. "Wanna meet me for dinner tonight? There must be at least one decent place to grab some grub in this sleepy town."

Hannah ignored Rocky. She pointed to Pearl and the cars. "It's time to tell your friends to skedaddle."

Officer Pam Larson drove in as far as possible. Hannah had never been so happy to see her.

"Whoa, Doll Face. Did you call the cops?" Rocky high-tailed it into the cottage and rounded up the others in less than a minute. On his way past Hannah, still bare-chested but with a black t-shirt draped over one shoulder, he held his thumb and pinky to his ear. "Nana's got my number. Call me."

"Yeah, right," Hannah mumbled under her breath. Maybe when the Atlantic freezes solid.

The five Cadillacs backed out leaving a cloud of dust and one police woman staring in disbelief. "I can't wait to hear the explanation of that, Ms. Holiday. After I have a chat with all your guests." Pam stared at Petunia grunting and rooting at the edge of the cottage. "Is that a pig?"

Pearl picked up Petunia. "She's a pot belly pig to be exact. Six months old and house trained."

"Is that so?" Pam crossed her arms and leaned against Pearl's red convertible. "Are you zoned for agriculture here, Ms. Holiday?"

"Pearl Martini is a guest and Petunia, her pet, will only be here temporarily," Hannah replied, hoping the fact that she didn't actually answer the question would go unnoticed by Pam.

"I'll keep that in mind." She checked her iPad. "Who's staying in your other cottages? I'd like to have a little chat with each person. Separately, of course." She glanced at Pearl. "Starting with you."

"Sherry Wolfe is staying in Cottage Three, and you spoke to the couple in Cottage Four yesterday—Aaron and Laura Masterson."

Pam made a few notes. "I'll use your office, Ms. Holiday. Follow me." Pam walked to Hannah's office without checking to see if anyone followed. Pearl didn't.

Hannah walked in behind Pam. The officer made herself comfortable at Hannah's desk and waited.

Hannah looked over her shoulder. "Um, Pearl went back into her cottage."

Pam pursed her lips and tapped her chin. "That's okay. You and I can chat first. Sit down." Pam waited for Hannah.

"I'll stand." She was furious that Pam took *her* seat at *her* desk and she wasn't going to let Pam intimidate her.

"Fine. Why were you and your sister at the marina this morning?"

"Just checking to see if my guest, Lenny DiMarco, ever returned to the marina. Alive."

"What did you find out?"

Hannah paused. She didn't want to get Chase in trouble if he had told Hannah something he wasn't supposed to. "Nothing, except a body was found. Can you tell me if it was Lenny?"

"It's not. We found photos of him in Lenny's car and the dead guy was definitely not Lenny. Much shorter and fatter."

"Who is it?"

Pam shrugged. "Beats me. May be awhile before he's identified. Pretty beat up from the rocks."

"You're still searching for another body?"

"We are." Pam rested her chin on her entwined fingers. "There were more photos."

Hannah froze. She didn't dare move or say anything. She knew in the pit of her stomach that she wouldn't like what Pam was about to tell her. More photos couldn't be good if Pam made a point of bringing it up.

Pam stood up. "Okay, how about you ask Ms. Martini to come in here. I'm dying of curiosity to find out who all those," she cleared her throat, "*gentlemen* were who rushed out of her cottage in such a hurry when I showed up. If I didn't know better, Ms. Holiday, I'd think you were letting some bad thugs rent Cottage Two." Pam cocked her head to one side in a challenge to Hannah.

Hannah refused to take the bait. She did not want to get into a pissing match with Officer Pam Larson. The probability was high that it wouldn't end well for Hannah.

Cal knocked on the door and poked his head in, his face dropping when he saw Hannah was with Pam. "Do you have a minute, Hannah? I need your advice on something."

"Sure do." She turned back toward Pam. "Will you be able to find the guests yourself?" Hannah asked in an overly friendly voice.

Pam stood up. "I'll manage. Oh, I almost forgot. I'd like to talk to your sister, too. Is she here?"

Hannah froze with her back to Pam. "Ruby hasn't been feeling well. I'll check if she's asleep."

"Really? She looked fine when I saw the two of you at the marina. Don't bother her now."

Hannah held the office door open for Pam before she followed Cal to the snack bar. "More problems?"

"Nope. Everything's going perfect. I've got one more beam to replace. You'll be able to call the building inspector to swing by tomorrow for the final check," Cal said with a satisfied grin on his face.

"So, what advice did you need?" Hannah bent down to look under the snack bar at the new beams.

"Chicken or steak?"

"What?" Hannah straightened, cocked her head, and looked at Cal. The edges of his blue eyes wrinkled and his lips curved into a devilish smile. Her heart fluttered which reminded her to slow down already and remember what was important.

"For dinner tonight. I'm hoping you'd like to join me on my boat for a bite to eat."

The thought of spending the evening with Cal tempted Hannah beyond everything at the moment *except* solving the problem about Lenny's disappearance. "There's a good chance that Ruby and Olivia will be staying with me tonight."

"Bring them along. You know I can't say no to Olivia, and Theodore was just telling me how much he's missed your little niece."

"Oh, really? Theodore, the stuffed bear, told you he misses Olivia?"

"Uh huh. So, what's the answer? Chicken or steak?"

Hannah laughed. Laughing felt good after all the problems from the past twenty four hours. "Neither."

Cal's face fell.

"You've put in so much time here helping me, I'll pick up a couple of pizzas so neither one of us has to spend time cooking. It's the least I can do."

"Okay, I can live with that compromise. Bring Ruby and Olivia if they want to come."

"They can eat outside so we can have some alone time," Hannah suggested.

Cal's grin widened and he leaned close to Hannah. "Maybe just Ruby."

"Hey Cal," one of his workers hollered. "Got a problem with this last beam. It's not sitting right. Something's in the way."

"Not what I want to hear," Cal mumbled. "I'll check with you about dinner before I leave," he called to Hannah as he hurried to find out what the problem was.

Hannah took a quick look out over the ocean. It helped to focus on the distant horizon, where the sky met the water, to keep everything in perspective. She needed to see the big picture instead of each little problem that kept piling up. Strive toward the big picture of being able to relax and enjoy the beautiful ocean spot that her Great Aunt Caroline left her.

She realized that she desperately needed to get the income stream moving faster than a trickle or she might not be able to stay here.

She urgently needed the snack bar to open on time.

And more than anything else, she had to figure out how to keep Ruby and Olivia safe.

Chapter 6

Olivia flitted around Hannah's cottage like a month old puppy. "Hurry up Hannah. What's the surprise? Are you coming too, Mom?"

Finally, Ruby was dressed after a long hot shower. She told Hannah she needed to wash away the memory of seeing Lenny. Not that it helped much. Especially since Hannah's plan was to take a walk toward the site of the capsized boat to look for clues. It was unlikely they would find anything after the police scoured the shoreline, but it couldn't hurt.

Hannah picked Olivia up and twirled her around. "The surprise? You want to know the surprise?"

"Yesssss!" Olivia screeched all the way around Hannah's spinning circle.

"Let's go. I have an interesting guest in Cottage Two."

Olivia's face fell. "That doesn't sound fun. Your guests are boring."

"Not this one. Nellie loves her already. Come on."

Hannah, with Olivia holding her hand and dancing next to her, led the way to Pearl's cottage. Nellie ran ahead, anxious to visit with her new friend. Ruby trailed behind with lead in her feet.

Pearl, in all her purple glory, emerged through the cottage door. Petunia, with her leash and harness, trotted out right next to her.

"A pig!" Olivia squealed as she dashed to embrace Petunia. "You didn't tell me your guest is a pig."

"A pot belly pig to be exact, dear. And who are you?" Pearl asked.

"This is Olivia," Hannah explained. "Can we take Petunia for a walk with us?" She hoped Pearl didn't ask any more questions about Olivia since Ruby was jumpy about who knew what about her until Lenny was found. Preferably, without the ability to stalk Ruby ever again.

"A walk? I suppose Petunia would love to join you. Let me get her walking outfit." Pearl returned inside. Ruby mouthed *walking outfit? Is she for real?*

They didn't have to wait long before Pearl returned with a colorful sunhat and Petunia's sunglasses. She handed the items to Hannah. "Just in case. She does sunburn easily."

Hannah gave Ruby the silent look they had always shared to mean *craaaazy* before she accepted the accessories and Petunia's leash. "We shouldn't be gone for too long."

"I'm meeting Rocky in town, so just keep Petunia until I get back," Pearl casually stated. "Oh. And don't feed her anything." Pearl lowered her voice and cupped her hand around her mouth, apparently so Petunia wouldn't hear what was coming next. "She's been gaining too much weight."

Again, Hannah gave her sister the silent look before she stepped away from Pearl with Petunia and Olivia at her side. Nellie dashed to the path beyond Cottage Four and Olivia pulled Petunia's leash away from Hannah.

The little girl looked up at her aunt. "Can I wear Petunia's hat and sunglasses until she needs them?"

"Great idea." Hannah pushed the sunhat over Olivia's French braids and handed her the pink sunglasses which Olivia slid onto her nose. Upside down.

Olivia and Petunia tried to catch up with Nellie but their strides were much shorter and slower than the golden retriever's long graceful bounds.

Hannah and Ruby walked in silence for several minutes, until Hannah blurted out, "What did you and Officer Larson talk about when she found you this afternoon?"

Ruby sighed and her shoulders sagged. "It wasn't good. She found photos of me and Olivia in Lenny's car."

"I was afraid of that. How did you explain it?"

"I lied." Ruby grabbed Hannah's arm and stopped walking. "I told her I had no idea who Lenny is. Pam mumbled something about probably a stalker."

"Are you sure there was nothing in the photos to link you with him?"

"With Olivia, no. I think he got those images when we were walking to or from school. He may not have figured out his connection to Olivia."

"So he *was* stalking you."

"In those photos, yes. But there was one that was kind of blurry that he must have taken when I met with him the other day. When I was walking back to my car."

Hannah started walking again. "I see this going one of two ways. The first is the best. For you. Lenny's body turns up and he's out of your life once and for all."

"And the other way?"

"He turns up alive and Pam will be off your back but Lenny might figure out that Olivia is his daughter."

"You're making a dangerous assumption, Hannah. What if Lenny has simply vanished into thin air? He's done it before."

Hannah could hear Olivia talking to Petunia. "And if you stay at Aunt Hannah's cottage, I'll get to see you all the time. Me *and* Nellie."

Another problem, Hannah told herself— Olivia must have missed the part that Petunia was only a guest. She hoped it didn't break Olivia's heart when Petunia left, like so many others in her life. She picked up the pace, pulling Ruby along with her. "I hear someone talking and I can't see Olivia."

The raced around the corner and laughed. Poor Sherry Wolfe was standing in the brush at the side of the path while Petunia stared at her. Olivia happily chatted to Sherry. "Don't be scared of Petunia. She's just a little pot belly pig." Olivia bent down to examine the pig's underside. "I don't know where the pot is but she's a sweet pig anyway. Do you have any pets? I want to get a cat but my mom says I have to wait until I'm six. I'll be six on April something. Mom? What day is my birthday?"

"Soon, honey. Let's let the woman finish her walk in peace."

Sherry glared at Hannah but managed to pat Olivia on the head as she jumped by Petunia.

"Nice walk, Sherry?" Hannah asked. "Did you see anyone along the beach?"

Sherry paused. "What? See anyone? Ah, no. Just all of you. Why are you being so nosy? Can't a person take a walk without being accosted?" She scurried away, her backpack slapping against her back with every footstep.

"That was a strange reaction," Ruby said as she stood looking backwards at Sherry's retreating back.

Hannah waved her hand, dismissing Sherry Wolfe's comments. "I think Petunia scared her out of her comfort zone. She's a retired teacher thinking about relocating to Hooks Harbor but I'm not sure Hooks Harbor is ready for someone like her, and it certainly looks like she's not ready for a neighbor like Petunia."

The path opened up to a rocky shoreline. "This is where Lenny's boat was found." Waves crashed into the big rocky point. Hannah shuddered. "I don't see how he could have survived. If the rocks didn't smash him to bits, the cold Atlantic would do him in."

"I wish I had your confidence, but you don't know Lenny. He's always got a plan. He's up to something. What about that map on his camera? We should study it some more and see if it ties in with this spot or somewhere else around here."

Hannah put her arm around Ruby's shoulders. "Now you're thinking. I knew this walk would be useful. I forgot about the map. How about we head back? Cal invited us all for dinner if you and Olivia want to come."

Olivia, with her big ears, heard that and jumped up and down. "Can we bring Petunia? Theodore would *love* Petunia."

"We'll have to check with Pearl. She's probably wondering where her pot belly pig is," Hannah told Olivia.

They all turned back to the trail. Petunia pulled Olivia off the path with her persistent rooting in the sandy dirt.

"It's better for her to root here than in front of the cottages," Hannah said as she took the leash from Olivia. "I'll try to guide her in the right direction while she's having her fun."

Petunia would have none of it. She wanted what she wanted and she pulled Hannah farther off the trail.

"What's that?" Hannah bent down to see what Petunia was after. "Someone buried some peanut butter cracker wrappers here." Hannah stuffed the trash in her pocket. "Petunia has a good nose."

Petunia kept working in the same area. "What's this?" She grabbed the sleeve of a turquoise colored t-shirt and pulled it free of the dirt. Hannah gasped. "This looks like the shirt Lenny wore the day he came to rent the cottage. Before he went to the marina." She held it up to show Ruby.

Ruby's face drained of color. "I told you. He's still alive."

Chapter 7

Ruby sagged into Hannah's comfy chair when they returned to Hannah's cottage. She begged off going to Cal's boat for dinner even though Olivia was thrilled with the plan and sat down to draw Cal a picture while she waited for Hannah to get ready to leave.

Pearl babied Petunia as if she had been gone for weeks instead of an hour. "Did you have a nice walk?" Pearl asked in a high pitched baby voice as she scratched Petunia's back. Petunia grunted with pleasure as she twisted her little body one way, then the other.

"I'll get caught up with some of your paperwork," Ruby said as she walked toward the door to Hannah's office. "I need to keep my mind busy."

Hannah nodded. "And study the photos?"

Ruby nodded. Grim-faced.

Hannah stashed the turquoise shirt in the back of her closet. She didn't have a plan. Yet.

"Okay, Olivia. Ready to roll?" Hannah tried to sound upbeat. She wanted to distract her from Ruby's problems.

Hannah and Olivia picked up pizza—a small cheese for Olivia and a large eggplant, mushroom, and onion for Cal and herself. Olivia was uncharacteristically quiet in the car, just gazing out the window and jiggling her feet.

Finally she turned to look at Hannah. "Is Mom going to move again?"

Hannah's antenna went up. This could be an innocent question since moving often was all that Olivia had ever known, or she might have picked up on something Ruby and Hannah talked about. "I don't think so, honey, why are you asking?"

"I like it here. With you and Cal and Petunia and Nellie. And Theodore."

"You know what Cal told me?"

Olivia shook her head.

"He thinks Theodore misses you. Cal has been busy and hasn't had much time for him lately."

A tear slid down Olivia's cheek. "Poor Theodore. It's no fun to be lonely. Maybe Theodore could visit with me for a while. We could keep each other company," she said hopefully.

"I think that's a wonderful idea." Hannah pulled into the Bayside Marina parking lot. "Ask Cal. I bet he'll say it's okay."

Hannah carried the pizza boxes with one arm and held Olivia's hand with the other as they walked down the dock to Cal's boat. Olivia pointed to the back of one boat and worked out the words—*"On the Rocks,"* she proudly read.

"I didn't know you could read already," Hannah said. "How about this next boat?" She pointed to the back of the boat next to Cal's before she even looked at the words.

"*Sink or Swim*," Olivia slowly sounded out. She looked up at Hannah. "Why would anyone choose to sink instead of swim?" Her five year old logic couldn't make any sense of those words.

The words gave Hannah a chill. "Kind of silly, isn't it?" Hannah said, moving Olivia forward. There was only one reason that Hannah could imagine sinking instead of swimming as a vision of Lenny's body floating in the ocean entered her brain. There was no choice in that situation.

"What does Cal's boat say? I can't figure out the first word," Olivia asked.

"Seas the Day," Hannah said.

Olivia reached her hand out and grabbed a fistful of air. "Here. This is all I can fit in my hand." She carefully attempted to transfer the air in her hand to Hannah. "Did you get it all?"

Hannah snapped her hand closed. "I sure did. Thanks."

Olivia leaped onto the back of Cal's boat without waiting for Hannah to help her. Her short legs barely made it across the open space and Hannah felt her breath catch. Without a word, she followed Olivia's example and realized that her niece was showing her how to seize this day without sinking. Clever girl.

"Who do I hear jumping onto my boat?" Cal's voice asked from inside the cabin. "Are those fish jumping aboard?"

"No, silly. It's me and Hannah. Hannah has the pizza so I jumped across all by myself. Where's Theodore? Hannah told me he's been lonely." Olivia looked up at Cal with big round innocent eyes.

"She did, did she? Well, she's right. I told Theodore that you were coming to visit and he's waiting up the ladder on my bed." Cal took the pizza boxes from Hannah and set them on his small table next to a couple of cold beers.

Olivia shimmied up the ladder. "There you are, Theodore. Would you like to come home with me for a visit?"

"Hmmm, sounds like my teddy bear has an admirer," Cal said. "Maybe it's time to pass him on to someone that needs him more than I do. What do you think, Hannah?"

"Olivia loves Theodore. She'd give him a good home for sure, and I think she's feeling a little insecure at the moment."

"About what?" Cal's voice was laced with concern.

Hannah slid pizza onto a plate for herself and whispered to Cal, "She asked me if her mom was going to move again." Hannah shook her head. "She's done *enough* moving. Olivia's in kindergarten now and it's time they put down some roots."

Cal poured a Sam Adams into a mug for himself and one for Hannah. "Why would Ruby move? She has a cute house. You're close to help out with Olivia. Is she getting enough freelance writing assignments for the paper?"

"Work isn't the issue. She's helping me, too. I can't keep up with the paperwork, and she's way more organized than I am." Cheese dripped down Hannah's chin after she bit the tip of the triangle off. Fanning her mouth she warned, "It's hot, be careful."

Cal drank some beer instead. "Why would she move, then? You didn't answer that part of my question."

Hannah set her pizza down and inhaled a deep breath. "I can't talk about it now with—" She nodded her head toward the loft. "Big ears, you know?"

Olivia, with Theodore tucked under her arm, descended the ladder from Cal's sleeping area. "I'm hungry."

"Well, slide right in here between us. I have a piece of cheese pizza all cooled off and ready for you. Is Theodore hungry too?" Hannah asked.

Olivia scrunched up her face and, with a serious voice, told Hannah, "He can't eat. He's only a teddy bear."

Cal hid his chuckle behind his hand. "Olivia, I've been thinking. Poor Theodore sits up on my pillow all day and I think he might like a change of scenery. Would you like to take him to your house for a visit?"

Olivia's eyes widened to the size of Theodore's round bear ears. She squeezed him tight. "Really?" She held Theodore in front of her face. "What do *you* think, Theodore?" She shook the teddy bear and made his head nod up and down. Olivia smiled. A big, happy smile. "Theodore says *yes*!"

"That's settled then," Cal said. He winked at Hannah.

Olivia gobbled down her pizza and climbed the ladder again with Theodore in her arms. "We're gonna look out the little window and watch the ocean," she said to anyone who was listening.

Cal helped himself to another slice of pizza and another cold beer. He held a bottle toward Hannah. She nodded. "Sure, why not? It's been a long day."

"You do look kind of stressed. Does it have something to do with your missing guest?" Cal kept his eyes on Hannah's face. She looked away. "Tell me what's going on. I want to help."

"I know, but it's not my secret to share."

"Fair enough." He stacked the plates and put them in the sink. "I'll wash these later after I walk you two beautiful ladies to your chariot."

Olivia leaned over the top of the ladder and scrunched up her face. "We don't have a chariot. We came in a car." She scooted down the ladder.

Cal rested his hand on Olivia's head. "Chariot is a fancy term for your car. Doesn't it sound like more fun?"

Olivia shrugged. "I dunno." She held Theodore tightly to her chest and skipped to the back of the boat. "You're coming to my house tonight. Hang on to me so you don't fall in the water."

"And you hang on to me so *you* don't fall in," Cal said as he caught up and held Olivia's hand.

They jumped from the back of Cal's boat to the dock and waited for Hannah to join them. She inhaled deeply. "What a beautiful clear night. Look at all those stars."

Olivia tilted her head back and counted as she stabbed her finger from star to star. She got to ten. "What's next?"

"Eleven," Hannah absentmindedly answered. What *is* next, she wondered, but numbers weren't on her mind at the moment.

Cal slipped his free hand around Hannah's waist and leaned toward her ear. "Don't forget, I'm always available if there's anything you want to talk about. Don't try to figure it out by yourself."

Hannah heard his words but remained silent, lost in her thoughts of what Lenny's disappearance could mean.

"Chase told me something interesting earlier," Cal said.

"Since when are you and Chase chatting buddies?" They walked toward Hannah's car leaning against each other.

"I ran into him when all the police were here and the helicopter was leaving for another search. He needed someone to complain to about how all the police activity was bad for his marina."

Hannah matched her pace to Cal's and waited for him to continue.

"He told me you and Ruby came by asking him if he had information about the body. It got him thinking and he remembered seeing the missing guy, Lenny, arguing with a short fat guy before he left in the boat."

Hannah stopped. Olivia ran ahead to the car and climbed in the front seat with Theodore.

"Short and fat? That's how Pam described the body of the dead guy they found. So the dead guy and Lenny were here at the marina together."

"Who is this Lenny guy? Do you know him? I thought he was just a random guest at the cottages," he said with an edge to his voice. Cal let go of Hannah's waist.

"That's what I thought, too," Hannah said, barely above a whisper. "Turns out I couldn't have been more wrong."

Cal's hand tightened on Hannah's arm. "Tell me what's going on. Are you in some kind of danger?"

She shook her head as she stared at Cal. "Ruby is."

Chapter 8

Light brightened Hannah's office window when she returned to her cottage and carried a sleepy five year old and a well-worn teddy bear inside.

"Did you have fun?" Ruby asked as she returned to the side of the cottage where Hannah lived and closed the office door.

Olivia's head rested on Hannah's shoulder but she managed to give her mom a smile and a nod. Hannah transferred Olivia to Ruby's arms and unrolled a camping mattress on the floor. "Olivia and Theodore can sleep here."

"Cal managed to part with his teddy bear?" Ruby smiled. She tucked the blanket around both Olivia and Theodore. Nellie curled up on the pad near Olivia's feet.

"He did." Hannah pulled her bedroom door almost closed. She left it opened a crack so Olivia wouldn't be scared if she woke up.

Hannah took a beer out of her fridge, handed it to Ruby, and offered her the leftover pizza. "I suppose you didn't eat anything while we were gone."

Ruby flipped the box top open and ate a piece using the box as her plate. "This isn't bad." She ate a second piece.

Hannah waited patiently for Ruby to fill her stomach before she brought up her conversation with Olivia. "She's worried you're planning to move again, you know."

Ruby drained the beer. "I don't want to leave but I have to."

Hannah jumped out of her chair and paced in her small room. "No! You can't keep doing this to Olivia. She's in school now. You have to stop running away."

Ruby's face fell into her hands and tears streamed down her cheeks. "What if he takes her away from me, Hannah?"

"Doesn't Olivia deserve to know who her dad is?"

Ruby stood up, walked into Hannah's office, and returned with her iPad. "I transferred the images from Lenny's camera. There's stuff on here you need to see." Ruby scrolled through the images, stopping at several. "Look at all these photos of me and Olivia. He's been stalking me for weeks at least. Possibly looking for a pattern in my daily routine. And this one shows a short fat guy. It looks like the same house where I met Lenny earlier this week." She stopped to stare at Hannah.

"Is there more?"

Ruby enlarged an image of a map. Hannah moved the iPad closer to her face. "I've seen something like this. Pearl has a map she claims came from Great Aunt Caroline. A treasure map. And Jack has one I found in Great Aunt Caroline's stuff right after I moved in."

They both jumped at the sound of a quiet knock on the cottage door. Ruby looked at Hannah, her eyes wide and her jaw clenched. "Who is it?" she whispered.

Hannah went to the door and cracked it slightly. "Oh, Jack, come on in." She pulled the door wider. Hannah heard Ruby let out her breath.

"I saw lights on. Is it too late to entice you to join me with some decaf and one of Meg's brownies? It's Caroline's recipe."

"Come on in. We were just," Hannah glanced at Ruby, "talking."

Jack set his coffee carafe on the table and waited for Hannah to get mugs, cream, and sugar. "Pam stopped by my house earlier."

Hannah's hand stopped midair on its way to pouring the coffee. She set the carafe back down and forgot about it.

"Yeah, she'll be stopping here tomorrow with more questions. For Ruby. She's pretty convinced that Ruby knows Lenny DiMarco. Want to tell me what's going on?" Jack finished pouring the coffee.

The sisters exchanged their look. Hannah nodded slightly. "Tell him, Ruby. Jack might have some good advice."

"Lenny is Olivia's dad," Ruby said in one rushed exhale.

Jack leaned forward. "Oh. You lied to protect Olivia."

"How do you know I lied?" Ruby demanded to know.

"Pam told me. She suspected it after finding so many photos of you and Olivia in Lenny's car. And you don't have a very strong poker face." He blew on his steaming coffee. "She's not happy about it but, under the circumstances, she'll probably understand. You know, the whole protective mama bear thing." He took a sip. "He's probably out of your life anyway. No one believes he could have survived in the cold water."

Another look passed between Hannah and Ruby.

Jack didn't miss it. "What else? Are you going to tell me he's not dead?" His eyes searched Ruby's face, then Hannah's. "Do you have evidence?"

Hannah walked to her closet and pulled the turquoise t-shirt out. "Lenny was wearing this the day he rented the boat."

Jack shrugged. "It could have washed ashore."

"And buried itself?" Hannah asked. "Petunia rooted it out several feet off the trail to the rocky point. Along with some peanut butter cracker wrappers." She threw the t-shirt on the table and pulled the wrappers from her jeans pocket. "I don't think this t-shirt buried itself."

Jack leaned back in his chair and folded his arms behind his head. "Interesting. Any idea what he might be up to? *If* he's still alive?"

Hannah leaned toward Jack. "Do you remember that treasure map I found in Caroline's stuff after I moved in? Do you still have it? Ruby thinks that's what brought Lenny here to Hooks Harbor."

He flicked his wrist. "Have you two lost your minds? A treasure map? Caroline liked to plant crazy ideas and watch people scramble for the answer. I think that treasure map is a giant hoax, and if she's watching from somewhere, she's having a good old laugh."

"You didn't answer the question. Do you still have it?"

"Sure I do. I'll dig it out when I get home." He stood up. "You two better get some sleep and figure out how you're going to explain all this to Pam. I'll come over early and make you some coffee—strong and dark. You'll need it."

"Jack? No one knew about Lenny and Olivia. Not even Lenny, as far as I know," Ruby said.

"If he didn't know about Olivia, what was he doing in Hooks Harbor?" Jack paused with his hand on the doorknob, his eyes on Ruby.

"The treasure map. He came searching for the treasure. I'm positive of that."

"So it's a coincidence that you just happened to be here too?" Jack shook his head. "Sounds fishy." He pulled the door closed quietly.

"He's right, you know," Hannah said. "In this whole big wide world, you and a buried treasure end up in the same place?"

Ruby scrolled back to the photo of the short fat guy and tapped the screen with her fingernail. "Do you think he could be the connection? We have to find out who he is."

Hannah sat back and sighed. "We won't get any information from Pam." She drummed her fingers on the table. "This is a long shot, but I'll talk to Pearl tomorrow. She knows people." Hannah put her fingers up and made air quotes around the word *people*.

Ruby's eyes narrowed. "What kind of people?"

"Remember you told me Lenny had connections to the mob?"

Ruby nodded.

"Jack told me that Pearl's first husband had ties to the mob, too. And he's here in town with some not too intelligent looking thugs. Never mind Pearl's grandson, Rocky."

Ruby smacked her forehead. "Rocky? I forgot to tell you. A guy named Rocky stopped in the office when you and Olivia were having dinner at Cal's boat. He said he was looking for Doll Face." Ruby smirked and wiggled her left eyebrow. "Is that you by any chance?"

Hannah groaned and rolled her eyes. "What did he want?"

"You. He was quite disappointed when I said you were gone. But he sat down, made himself at home, and took a pack of cigarettes from his rolled up t-shirt sleeve. Who still does that?"

"At least he had his shirt on and didn't strut in like some kind of peacock on the prowl," Hannah said.

Ruby laughed. "He does have the strut down pretty good. What's his story anyway?"

"I might actually have to be nice to him. Pearl, in her completely unsubtle way, let me know she thinks her grandson would be the perfect match for me. It might be the key to getting her help."

Ruby laughed so hard she made a mad dash for the bathroom and yelled through the closed door. "All that beer and coffee was not a good combination for my bladder."

"Keep laughing and you'll be the one that has to cozy up to Rocky to get information from Pearl."

The laughter stopped. Almost. One muffled snort broke the silence.

When Ruby returned, she said, "He is sort of cute in a, what do you call it?" She put her finger on her chin. "I've got it, a harmless hoodlum kind of way. I don't think he's the type that will want to listen to you read poetry while you sit under the stars with him."

Hannah playfully slapped her sister. "Laugh all you want but he could end up helping us."

"I can't believe you'd use that poor love-struck puppy to your advantage. Reminds me of how you treated that boy in high school."

Hannah's mouth fell open. "That's such an exaggeration. He helped me with my homework and I—"

"Right! You sat next to him in study hall. While he *did* your homework. "

"Okay. You win." Hannah stopped laughing and got serious. "This is different. This is important for you and Olivia."

"I know. I've been trying to distract myself by picking on you. I hope your plan gets us somewhere."

Nellie started to bark.

"Mommy?" Olivia's tiny voice called from the bedroom. "Someone's outside the window."

Hannah reached Olivia before Ruby. She sat in the middle of the mattress clutching Theodore, her eyes round circles.

"What did you see, sweetheart," Hannah calmly asked Olivia as she held the little girl in her lap.

"I heard something. It woke us up." She squeezed Theodore tighter.

"What should we do?" Ruby whispered.

"I'm sure it's nothing," Hannah said, trying to sound confident. "You stay here with Olivia and I'll take a look.

Hannah clutched her big flashlight and went outside with Nellie at her side. Nellie charged off the porch, leaving Hannah alone. Her eyes adjusted to the darkness. She moved the flashlight beam slowly along the edge of the cottage. Her heart raced.

"Don't shoot," a voice teased. "Is that the weapon of choice in this hick town?"

Hannah moved the beam of light from the two boots about five feet in front of her, up to two hands held palms out, and then to Rocky's face. A big, goofy grin stretched from one ear to the other.

"What are you doing outside my cottage? You . . . " she was at a loss for the right word. "Were you looking in my windows?"

"Whoa, slow down, Doll Face. I'm looking for Petunia. She's out here somewhere and Nana won't go to bed until I get the pig back inside."

Hannah felt her body relax. It was only Petunia that scared Olivia. "I'm sure Nellie will find her."

"Nellie? That crazy dog that almost ran me down? Who keeps an animal like that, anyway?"

"She's trained to kill on my command. She's *my* weapon of choice," Hannah hissed as she jabbed the flashlight toward his chest.

That wiped the grin off Rocky's face. He backed away from Hannah. "I don't mean no harm, Doll Face. Don't sic that animal on me."

Fortunately, Nellie trotted back toward Hannah with Petunia at her side. She looked up at Rocky and woofed. He backed away. Hannah covered her mouth so Rocky wouldn't see her laughing.

"She ain't gonna bite me, is she?"

"Not if you don't come near me. She's extremely protective."

"No problem with that. I saw that carpenter dude at the marina and he told me to stay away from you. You aren't even my type. I was only asking you out to please Nana."

"Not your type? You have a *type*?" Hannah never felt so insulted. Rejected by Rocky Amato—a preening, cigarette smoking, full of himself hoodlum. Ouch. "Maybe I could have been a bit friendlier." She lowered the flashlight and patted her leg for Nellie to stand next to her. "I could use your help with something."

"Oh yeah? I get it. Now you need me so you'll be nice." He flicked his wrist dismissively. "Forget it, Doll Face." Rocky hooked the leash on Petunia and led her past Hannah to Cottage Two.

"Come on, Nellie. Tomorrow *has* to be better than today." Hannah double checked that all the doors were locked when she got back inside. Just in case.

Chapter 9

Hannah woke up to the sound of someone pounding on her door. Nellie wasn't barking.

"Come in," she hollered as she slipped a sweatshirt over her pj's.

The door rattled but didn't open. "It's locked. Since when do you lock your door?" Hannah let Jack in and relieved him of the bag he carried. "I'll make coffee here."

"There's more than coffee in this bag. What else did you bring?"

Hannah hefted the bag up and down, feeling the weight before she attempted to unpack the bag. Jack snatched it away. "A surprise." He looked around the room. "Where are your guests? Didn't Ruby and Olivia stay here last night?"

Hannah tilted her head toward the closed bedroom door. "They must be awake by now with all the racket you made."

Jack checked the time. "The school bus will be here in a half hour." Jack started the coffee and took plates from Hannah's cupboard.

"I forgot." Hannah cracked the bedroom door and called quietly, "Ruby. Olivia. Time to get out of bed. Jack brought a surprise."

Olivia appeared in two seconds flat, bright eyed and happy.

Ruby plopped herself into a chair, eyes puffy and only half opened. "You kicked me all night, Hannah. I forgot what a restless sleeper you are."

"Jack's got coffee brewing. I'll make Olivia's lunch for school so you can sit and take your time waking up."

"Here's my surprise," Jack said. He put a large canning jar of homemade granola on the table. "Oatmeal, nuts, and coconut, sweetened with maple syrup. I also have," he reached his hand back into the bag, "cider donuts." He pulled one from the bag with a great flourish. "Someone here likes these if I remember correctly."

"I do. I do." Olivia bounced in her chair. "Can I have two?" She quickly added, "Please."

Jack's eyes crinkled at the edges. "You're not going to feed them to that bear, are you?"

Olivia looked at Theodore sitting next to her. "You're silly. Theodore doesn't eat donuts."

Hannah poured Olivia a glass of milk and gave her one donut. "I'll save the other one for an after school snack. Hurry up and I'll walk you to the bus stop." She set a mug of coffee in front of Ruby and a bowl. "Want some of Jack's granola?"

Ruby sipped the coffee. "Ahhh. This is the best." She helped herself to the granola. "Don't forget to help Olivia brush her teeth."

"Right." Hannah and Olivia reappeared, Olivia with her favorite red long sleeve t-shirt on with a picture of a teddy bear, and Hannah carrying her niece's backpack with

Theodore safely tucked inside with her lunch.

Hannah also carried her coffee. "Oops. We've got to run. I see the bus."

The bus stopped and waited for Olivia to climb on. She waved to Hannah through the window as the bus pulled away.

Nellie followed Hannah back toward her cottage. "I have to figure out how to keep Ruby from moving again," Hannah said to her dog. "Olivia is so happy here."

A scream pierced the morning air making Hannah's arm jerk and her coffee splash all over her cream colored shirt. What met her eyes made her laugh out loud, distracting her from the hot coffee seeping through her shirt. Sherry ran away from the snack bar, holding one arm above her head. Petunia followed at a trot. Sherry kept looking over her shoulder but Petunia was intent on catching her and getting whatever treat Sherry refused to share.

Another hysterical scream followed the first, before Sherry caught up to Hannah.

"Call 911," she managed to say between her gasps for air.

"Did she hurt you?" Hannah asked, worried that Petunia did some damage to Sherry besides to her mental health.

"She? How do you know the murderer is a she?" Sherry's face was as white as the foam on the waves.

"Murderer?"

Sherry pointed toward the snack bar which was jacked up on one end, waiting for the final new beam to be put in place. She pulled Hannah closer and jabbed her finger toward the corner of the shack.

What met Hannah's eyes made the color drain from her face, too. A bright green sneaker, attached to a leg, stuck out. She looked at Sherry. "Who is that?"

"I don't know, but he's not moving. When I walked by a minute ago, the pig came out from under the shack. Do you think the pig did it?"

Hannah moved closer. More came into view—two bright green canvas sneakers, no socks, and the bottom of the hem of a pair of plaid shorts. Something about the shorts looked familiar. Was it the turquoise color? She dialed 911 and managed to tell the dispatcher that there was a body under her snack bar before she leaned over and threw up Jack's delicious coffee.

By the time her stomach was empty, Cal, who had just driven in, jumped from his truck and rushed to Hannah's side. Jack and Ruby were only seconds behind. "We heard screams," Jack said as they all huddled around Hannah.

Pearl came running and waved her arms. "I heard someone scream. Is Petunia all right? She's so smart, she figured out how to open the door. Oh, there you are, you naughty girl." Pearl crouched down and made cooing talk to the pot belly pig.

Hannah straightened and pointed behind her to the green sneakers.

"Is it Lenny?" Ruby asked, her hand covering her mouth.

"Who's Lenny?" Pearl wanted to know. "And what's he doing under that building?"

"Sherry found him," Hannah said. "Or maybe it was Petunia." Hannah looked left and right. "Where did Sherry go?"

Rocky joined the growing crowd, shirtless and running his fingers through his hair. "Geez, can't a guy sleep in around here without so much racket?"

Aaron, with his arm around his wife's shoulders, walked toward their car. "What's going on?" he asked before his eyes registered the body and his mouth dropped open.

Jack kneeled next to the legs and inched partway under the raised floor of the snack bar. "I don't feel any pulse. And from the look of this knife sticking out of his back, I don't think it's an accident either." He looked up at the waiting faces. "Anyone have any idea who this is?"

Ruby dropped down next to Jack and peered under the snack bar. Silently, she looked at Hannah and nodded her head slightly.

Hannah pulled Ruby back. Sirens wailed closer and closer.

Jack whispered to Hannah, "I saw Ruby nod to you. If it's Lenny, that will take care of Ruby's problem with him."

"Maybe, unless your daughter makes the connection between Ruby and Lenny. The lie Ruby told Pam about not knowing him will be a huge problem. Especially now."

"I see where you're going. Let's hope that doesn't happen."

"Then her problems escalate significantly. Like, she could be the prime suspect." Hannah sighed. She felt an arm on her shoulder.

"What's the matter, Doll Face? Never saw a dead guy before?"

Hannah jerked away from Rocky. "You were roaming around outside last night.

Maybe it was you sticking a knife in his back."

"Whoa. What's up with you? Can't a guy offer some comfort without being accused of murder?"

Cal stepped between Hannah and Rocky, putting *his* arm around Hannah. "Back off." Cal glared at Rocky.

Police cruisers raced into the driveway, stirring up a cloud of dust.

Sherry tapped Hannah on her shoulder. "I'm checking out of this loony bin. I want to settle my bill."

"Sorry. No one's going anywhere yet," Officer Pam Larson said to the group in general. "Not till I figure out what's happened. So, who called in a body?"

Hannah stepped forward.

"You, Ms. Holiday? Why are you always in the middle of the drama in Hooks Harbor? Show me what you found."

Hannah felt a comforting pat on her arm from Cal as she showed Pam the legs sticking out from under the snack bar.

"Did you touch anything?"

Hannah shook her head.

Jack approached his daughter and offered an air of calm. "I checked for a pulse."

Pam turned around to address the group—Hannah, Ruby, Cal, Jack, Pearl, Rocky, Aaron, Laura, and Sherry. "I'll need statements from each of you, so make yourselves comfortable." She waved her hand toward the ocean. "Enjoy the view while you wait."

More police cars, fire trucks, an ambulance, and every volunteer in town descended on Hannah's small snack bar. Yesterday was terrible, but today was already turning into a nightmare and it wasn't even ten o'clock in the morning. She looked at her poor snack bar waiting for the last beam to be replaced. It looked like it was impossible that she'd be able to open on time as she watched Pam unroll the yellow police tape.

"This couldn't be much worse," Hannah heard Ruby whisper in her ear. "What am I going to tell Pam? If I continue the lie, and she knows it's a lie, I'll look guilty. But if I tell her I lied and why, I'll *still* look guilty."

"You have an alibi—you, me, and Olivia were all sleeping in the bedroom together."

Ruby stood wringing her hands. "I went outside after you fell asleep. Just to sit and listen to the waves. The sound relaxes me."

"Pam doesn't have to know that."

"I think Rocky saw me. He was outside too."

"Where?"

"By the snack bar."

A piece of paper blew up against Hannah's leg. She picked it up. "I hate it when people just throw their trash on the ground." She glanced at it quickly, then turned away from everyone and grabbed

Ruby's arm "Look at this. We have to compare this to the map on Lenny's camera. Was he under the snack bar looking for the treasure?"

Hannah paced and Ruby clenched her hands. Cal worked on the picnic tables for outside the snack bar. Jack tried to follow his daughter around, giving her advice about what to look for until she told him to get lost.

Finally, Pam rounded everyone up to question them one by one. Alone in Hannah's office. Starting with Sherry.

While Hannah waited for her turn, she talked to Jack. "Look what I found." She passed him the folded up map. "Don't let anyone else see it."

Jack sat on a big rock at the edge of the parking area. His eyes met Hannah's after he spent a minute looking at the front and back, then the front of the map again. "Where'd you find this?"

"I thought it was a piece of trash blowing in the wind. Should I tell Pam?"

Jack rubbed his chin. "You should come clean with her. She'll find out everything eventually. Ruby too. This so-called buried treasure could be key to the murders."

"Murders? What are you talking about?" Hannah's eyes narrowed.

"The other guy? Found yesterday morning? He didn't drown. It was in the news this morning."

Hannah blinked. "How did he die?"

"Stabbed."

Chapter 10

Petunia trotted her little feet right through the middle of all the detectives and disappeared under the snack bar.

"Oh dear," Hannah heard Pearl say to Rocky. "I better get over there and retrieve Petunia before she upsets someone."

"Too late for that," Jack said to Hannah and Ruby, with a smile plastered on his face. "This should be interesting."

Pearl, with her flowing colorful muumuu streaming behind, marched over to the group of detectives. "I need to get my little Petunia."

"Huh?"

Pearl's brows shot up and her mouth dropped open. "Are you deaf? I have to get my Petunia." She pointed to the snack bar. "She's under there."

The second detective took Pearl's arm, firmly, and pulled her away. "What are you talking about? This is a murder scene. You can't go over there and contaminate the area."

"Hey, there's a pig coming out from under the floor. Where'd that pig come from?" the first detective shouted.

Pearl stomped her foot. "That's Petunia. If you had listened to me in the first place, you'd know that. Keep your voices down or you'll scare her."

The two detectives stared at each other, obviously at a loss for words about Petunia and, most likely, Pearl, too. "Okay lady, the pig's gotta go. I'll have to shoot her." He slipped his handgun from his holster.

"NO!" Pearl shrieked and lunged at the detective. "You'll have to shoot me, too."

Without thinking, Hannah rushed toward Petunia, upset that the detective even considered shooting the defenseless pig. In one scoop, she had Petunia in her arms and carried the squealing pig away from the snack bar. "You ought to be ashamed," she scolded the detective.

"Well, get it out of here. Next time, I won't give a warning." The detective glared at Hannah. "What's your name?"

"Hannah Holiday," she said loud and clear, but knowing deep down that this would come back to haunt her.

"Oh, Petunia. Are you all right?" Pearl glared at the group of detectives. Hannah could see that she was shaking with anger. "Hannah, you saved my baby. I'll be indebted to you forever." Pearl took Petunia and kissed her head. She attached the leash and walked back to Rocky. "Are you just a dumb coward? Why didn't you rush in and save Petunia?"

Rocky flicked his wrist. "It's only a pig. We coulda had her for dinner."

Pearl slapped Rocky on the cheek. "You stupid kid. You'd better watch your tongue or—"

Rocky cut her off and hissed, "Be quiet Nana before you say something—" His eyes darted to all the other people watching their drama. "Before you say something you can't take back." The scent of sweat lingered in the air as he stomped away from Pearl and passed close to Hannah.

Sherry left the office and headed straight for Hannah. "You've certainly made a mess of my vacation. I wanted a scenic quiet spot to relax and," she waved her hand around, "all it is here is chaos, pigs, and murder! Don't expect me to pay for this. I'm letting you know right now that I'm demanding a refund."

"So you'll be checking out? I'll refund the unpaid balance," Hannah said, trying to remain calm.

"No, I'm not checking out. I'm not allowed to leave this . . . this . . . this *joke* of a vacation paradise. I expect a refund for the whole week I prepaid." Sherry stood with one hand on her hip and jabbed the finger of her other hand in Hannah's face.

"Unbelievable," Hannah replied under her breath as she turned her back on Sherry. What had she gotten herself into, dealing with psycho guests like this nut case? Was it true that the customer was always right? Hannah didn't think so. Not in this case when the events were completely out of her control.

Pam motioned for Hannah to join her in the office. "Not how I expected to start my day. How about you, Ms. Holiday?" Pam closed the door behind Hannah.

Hannah didn't even feel that comment warranted an answer so she sat and waited.

Pam sat in Hannah's chair with her elbows on Hannah's desk and her hands clasped together. "You found the body?" Pam stared.

"Technically, I think it was Petunia who found the body."

"The pig?"

"Yes."

Pam jotted down a quick note.

Hannah imagined it said something like, *smart aleck witness, probably the murderer.*

"How did the pig get loose?" Pam leaned back in the chair. "I was under the impression that the pig would be under control while it was a," she cleared her throat, "a guest here."

"Apparently, Petunia figured out how to open the cottage door. It won't happen again," Hannah promised.

Pam's left brow rose. "I hope not." She paused.

The silence made Hannah nervous. What did Pam already know?

Pam leaned forward. "You were the first *person* to find the body?"

"No. That would be Sherry Wolfe, my guest staying in Cottage Three. I heard a scream and assumed Sherry was startled by Petunia until she pointed to the legs sticking out from under the snack bar."

"But *you* called 911."

"I did. Sherry told me to call."

Pam scribbled some more notes.

Blames other people for actions, Hannah imagined Pam writing.

"Do you know who the deceased is, Ms. Holiday?"

Ahh, Hannah thought, now Pam was getting down to the nitty gritty. She sighed. "I believe it's Lenny DiMarco, my guest who was supposed to be staying in Cottage Two. The guest who rented the boat that capsized."

Pam pursed her lips. "And why do you *believe* it's Mr. DiMarco? Did you crawl under the shed and get a good look at him?"

"No. The shorts were familiar and—"

Pam dipped her head and looked at Hannah over the rim of her glasses. "And what, Hannah?"

The interruption and name switch was not lost on Hannah. Was Pam trying to sound friendlier to get more information? Who knew, but it was time for Hannah to come clean. She sighed and looked at her hands. "Ruby recognized him."

"Okay, now we're getting somewhere." Pam jotted down a few more comments. "Do you want to keep playing this cat and mouse game or are you going to tell me everything you know? I *will* find out eventually, and if your sister is in trouble, the sooner we get to the bottom of this mess, the better for her."

"Honestly, I don't know much. Ruby only told me that she knew Lenny a couple of days ago. She's afraid of him but it's her story to share. I do have something else though."

"Lenny DiMarco's camera?" Pam asked.

"Well, yes. He left it in here." Hannah pointed behind the chair Pam sat in to a black camera bag. "But there's more." She pulled the folded paper from her pocket. "I found this outside a few minutes ago." She smoothed the map out on her desk and slid it close to Pam. "I think this is what brought Lenny to Hooks Harbor and possibly what he was looking for under my snack bar."

Pam studied the map. "A treasure map? Are you daft?"

"Maybe, maybe not. Your dad has a map like this that I found in my Great Aunt Caroline's things after I moved in. He planned to study it but I think it's been forgotten until now."

Pam flicked the map away. "I'm more interested in your guests. What can you tell me about Pearl Martini and her grandson? That was an interesting crew visiting her the other day. Not exactly the type of visitors Hooks Harbor is used to." Pam tilted her head. "I'm not done looking into their stories."

"Pearl was a friend of Great Aunt Caroline's when they were kids. Jack remembers her."

"And?"

"She has a treasure map, too. She claims Caroline sent it to her." Hannah leaned forward. "But here's the weird part. She got the letter with the map a year *after* Caroline died."

"So she told you?"

"That's right. At the time I had no reason *not* to believe her. Your father told me Pearl's first husband, Tony Amato, had ties to the mob. And he's in town, too. Doesn't it seem like too much of a coincidence that all these people arrived with the same goal in mind?"

"What goal? To kill Lenny DiMarco?"

"No. To find a buried treasure."

Pam looked at Hannah for several seconds before she started to laugh. "You're joking, right? I really don't have time for this baloney." Pam stood up. "Send your sister in next, Ms. Holiday."

Hannah stared in disbelief. Officer Pam Larson never liked Hannah from the first day she met her, but this was important information connected to a murder investigation. How could she be so flippant and dismissive about it? Ruby was headed for serious trouble if her freedom depended on Pam to connect all the dots to solve Lenny's murder.

Pearl owed Hannah a favor for saving Petunia's life, and now she was more determined than ever to cash in on it.

Chapter 11

Friday morning dragged into Friday afternoon with little hope of the police clearing out before the school bus dropped Olivia off from school. Finally, Officer Pam Larson finished questioning everyone. Lenny's body was gone but the yellow police tape remained around the snack bar. The yellow tape of death for Lenny DiMarco *and* Hannah's snack bar grand opening.

Ruby was despondent. She told Pam everything—the truth about her relationship with Lenny; that Lenny was Olivia's dad; that she had visited Lenny, at his request, earlier in the week; and how she spent the last five years running away from him. "It's not looking good," she told Hannah. "Every time Pam scribbled down some notes, it felt like a nail sealing my fate as the prime murder suspect."

Hannah squeezed Ruby's shoulder. "You had to come clean with Pam and there's no time to dwell on it. Let's move on. I invited Pearl over for coffee. We need to get her on board with your situation and find out who the short fat guy is. Pearl owes me." Hannah measured coffee for her coffee machine and got it started.

Ruby stayed slumped in the chair. "Olivia will be out of school soon so I'll take her back to our house and stay out of your way. I don't want her to get wind of any of this Lenny mess. I'll have to explain it to her someday, but I can't think about that conversation at the moment."

"Before you go, let's look through all the photos you downloaded from Lenny's camera. Pam took the camera bag and I forgot to tell her we kept copies of the images." Hannah grinned. "Oops, my bad."

Meg knocked on the partly opened door and the smell of seafood filled the room as she entered. "I brought you some food. With all that police tape around the snack bar, we may as well dig into these lobster rolls so they don't go to waste."

Hannah imagined the taste of the sweet lobster morsels as soon as Meg mentioned it. Her mouth watered. "You always drop in at the right time with something delicious to eat."

The three women sat around Hannah's table. Eating occupied their mouths for several minutes. Hannah placed the last quarter of her lobster roll on her plate, sat back, and sighed. "Oh man. That's a special treat. How did you know that was exactly what we needed now, Meg?"

Meg chuckled. "Everyone's the same. Food distracts us from all the stress and worry in our lives. If I wasn't always on my feet running all over the place, this," she patted her own stomach, "would be out here with all the comfort eating I do." Her arms extended in a circle in front of her lap.

"Yeah, right. You'll never have a weight problem. You and your twin brother Michael couldn't put on weight if you tried. I think you both must have the skinny gene," Hannah said with envy lacing her voice.

"Speaking of Michael," Meg said after she licked her fingers. "He told me some interesting characters have been hanging around his Pub and Pool Hall. He made sure to tell me to mention it to you. Seems he overheard your name pop up in a couple of the conversations."

"Oh? They wouldn't be scruffy mobster creeps by any chance? Four older men driving Cadillacs and one young stud who thinks his only job here on the planet is to drive women crazy?"

Ruby stood up. "Who could you be describing, Hannah? Is Rocky Amato working his charms on you? I thought I saw you flirting with him earlier." She laughed as she walked to the door. "I wish I didn't have to leave this fascinating conversation, but the bus is almost here. Call me later and fill me in." She waved on her way out.

Meg watched Hannah. "You seem to know who Michael was referring to. Quite the description, especially about the young stud. Friends of yours?" Meg asked.

"I know who Michael was talking about, but I wouldn't even go as far as to say I *know* them. And they certainly are no friends of mine. You know the woman in Cottage Two? Pearl Martini?"

Meg nodded. "Can't miss her with that purple hair and red sports car. And her pig. Is that mob with her?"

"Mob is right. I've heard they actually have ties to the mob, or at least, Pearl's ex-husband *had* ties. What were they doing at the pool hall?"

Meg shrugged. "It's a great place for creeps like them to hang out without bringing too much attention to themselves. Michael might not have paid as much notice if your name hadn't come up. Several times."

Hannah opened Ruby's iPad. "Let me show you something. I think this is the key to all that's happening." Hannah brought up the images of the map.

Meg slid her reading glasses from the top of her head down to rest on her nose. "I'd be lost without these. Okay, let me take a look at this." She pulled the iPad closer. "This looks familiar. Did Caroline have a map like this?"

"She did. Jack has it now. What do you think? Did Caroline ever talk about a treasure buried around here?" Hannah leaned closer to Meg to keep her eye on the map while Meg studied it.

Meg pulled her glasses off and chewed on one arm of their arms. "You know? She did mention something, but more in an off-handed, joking way. As I recall, she said something like—*wouldn't it be funny to convince people there was a buried treasure around here? What scoundrels would that attract?* I thought it was a gimmick she concocted to bring in more business."

"Looks like it worked. I wonder if she expected it to bring in a murderer, too," Hannah said. She flipped the cover over the iPad and pushed her chair away from Meg.

"We might be able to find out something interesting at the Pub and Pool Hall." Meg grinned at Hannah. "Are you thinking what I'm thinking?"

"Probably. Tonight would be just perfect to make a visit. Check out the local flavors, and the not-so-local trash."

"What time should I pick you up?" Meg asked.

"Nine? I've got to talk to Pearl Martini and I hope she can answer some questions. She arrived here with one of these treasure maps, too. I'm beginning to think that Great Aunt Caroline had a plan. I just haven't figured out the details. Yet."

Meg cleaned up the lobster roll wrappers. "What about your grand opening?"

Hannah held both hands out to her sides, palms up. "Not much I can do. Pam doesn't give one hoot about my problems. She's probably secretly happy to be ruining my opening."

"I have an idea."

"Spit it out." Hannah leaned forward again, anxious to hear Meg's suggestion.

"Michael has a kitchen at the pool hall. How about serving lobster rolls, clam chowder, and Caroline's famous slaw over there? You'll attract all the locals, maybe some tourists, and, mostly likely, the motley crew of gangsters. Michael will love the exposure. He'll sell lots of beer. You could even raffle off something."

"You've given this some real thought." Hannah flicked the end of her braid on her cheek.

"Yeah." She nodded. "Raffle off a weekend in one of your cottages. The whole event could benefit the library. Cal's sister told me they don't have any money for new books."

"I like this idea except it will be a big hit in my pocketbook. I don't know if I can swing it."

"Let me worry about that, too. I can scrounge up some donations. We'll make it work out for you, Michael, *and* the library. Are you in?"

Hannah paused, considering how much this little venture might cost her. "I'm in. With one condition."

"Oh boy. I'm sure I won't like it."

"How about," Hannah leaned toward Meg in a conspiratorial manner. "How about we raffle off the original, the one and only, treasure map from Great Aunt Caroline."

Meg roared with laughter. "Are we bringing her back to life to spook everyone?"

"I only care about spooking out the killer before Ruby gets charged with Lenny's murder. Or worse—someone else ends up with a knife in their back."

"All because of a silly treasure map?"

"There are at least six people in town I'm betting don't think it's a silly map. And that number was eight a couple of days ago. Care to make a guess as to how many more will be killed off?"

"As long as those scumbags keep killing each other, it cleans up the gene pool." Meg laughed.

Hannah slapped her arm. "You are one bad influence, Meg. Now, get out of here before Pearl shows up. I don't want to scare her off before I convince her to help me."

"With what?" Meg narrowed her eyes and studied Hannah's face.

"I want to know who that first victim is." Hannah filled Meg in on Ruby's background with Lenny. "Maybe the short, fat, now-dead guy is the connection between Lenny and the killer."

"You better be careful. How do you know you can trust Pearl?"

"I saved Petunia from being shot by one of the detectives this morning. She owes me."

Meg shook her head. "You are treading into dangerous waters, Hannah. I hope your Great Aunt Caroline doesn't regret starting her little joke about the buried treasure."

"It's a bit late for her to regret much of anything. Unfortunately. And I have to clean up the damage. Somehow."

Chapter 12

With Meg helping Jack find the *original* map that he had stored someplace, Hannah brought her attention back to Ruby's iPad and the images from Lenny's camera.

Something caught her eye in the photo. A set of knives, with one missing, rested on a table in the photo of the short fat guy. Hannah zoomed in on it. Was the missing knife the murder weapon?

She cropped the photo and printed the image of the short fat guy so she'd have something to show Pearl. The knife would have to wait. Hannah was positive that Officer Pam Larson would *not* miss that detail.

The sound of little feet trotting up her porch steps spurred Hannah to close the iPad and move it out of the way. Pearl, with a tiny bit less bravado than was her usual manner, tapped on the door. "Hellooo? Hannah?"

"Come on in, Pearl. Are you hungry? I have a delicious lobster roll for you if you're interested. It's supposed to be my signature food at the snack bar grand opening, but . . ." She shrugged her shoulders and sighed. "That's not happening on schedule."

"Oh dear." Pearl made herself comfortable at Hannah's table. Petunia rooted around the room, digging in Nellie's dog bed. "How can I help?"

Hannah placed the lobster roll in front of Pearl. Even though she didn't say she wanted it, who could resist? Tender chunks of fresh lobster meat, without all the work of cracking open the shell of the whole crustacean was a win-win. Hannah also had treats on hand for Petunia—a couple of grapes for her, and a homemade dog biscuit for Nellie.

"I'd love a cup of coffee too, dear. If it's no trouble."

Hannah poured two mugs and joined Pearl at the table. "I'm hoping you can help me." Hannah slid the image of the short fat guy across the table toward Pearl. "Any idea how to find out who this is?"

Pearl took a big bite of the lobster roll as she studied the image. "I've seen this guy before." She set the paper down, tilted her head, and looked up at Hannah. "But I'm not sure where. Why?"

Hannah sensed that Pearl was hiding something. *Did* she know who the short fat guy was? "How did you *really* get that map from Caroline, Pearl? And why did you show up in Hooks Harbor now? A year after Caroline died?"

Pearl sputtered and coughed, pretending her coffee went down her windpipe but Hannah could tell it was all for show. "You know, Hannah, you remind me a lot of your Great Aunt Caroline. No beating around the bush, just straight for the jugular. Let me tell you something you probably don't know about her."

Hannah leaned back, wondering if what Pearl was about to tell her was fact or fiction.

"I was always in Caroline's shadow." She fluffed her hair. "You might find that hard to believe, but it's true. Caroline had all the self-confidence in the world and I was always filled with self-doubt. She didn't need a red sports car to get attention. Or a cute pot belly pig to keep her company. Caroline knew what she wanted and she got it. Always."

"What does all that have to do with the guy in the photo?"

"I'm getting to that. It was maybe a year and a half ago, or a little more, I'm not sure. Anyway, I came here to visit Caroline. I know. I told you I hadn't seen her for years. No one knows I visited. Caroline suspected she wouldn't be around for too many more years and she wanted to be sure this business didn't just crumble and disappear."

Hannah nodded.

"She had a plan to get visitors to come to town. Bring in some business. Have a little fun."

"The treasure map," Hannah guessed.

"Right. The treasure map. And she let me take on the project. She had the idea but not the energy for the planning. The only stipulation was to wait until after she died."

"You mailed the letter with the map to yourself?"

"Sort of. The short fat guy in the photo you just showed me did some work for Caroline. On the side. Under the table. She didn't want anyone to associate him with her. He mailed it for me. And the other maps too. For a real live treasure hunt."

"How many maps are out there?" Hannah was skeptical of Pearl's story.

Pearl shrugged. "I'm not sure. But Caroline kept the original." She leaned toward Hannah with a glint in her eyes. "So, we can help each other. You want to know who that guy is and," she leaned back with a satisfied grin, "I want the original map."

Alarm bells clanged in Hannah's head and her stomach did a flip-flop but she forced herself to keep her face neutral. "Interesting proposition. I'll think about it."

Pearl's eyes widened. "So you have it?"

"No."

"Oh. Well, the deal's off then." She wiped her hands together for emphasis.

"I know where it is." Hannah decided to use her trump card to flush out the rest of Pearl's scheme. By now, Hannah was convinced Pearl was up to no good and was only out for the treasure. For herself. Apparently, Great Aunt Caroline never shared the hoax part of her buried treasure plan.

Pearl's hand slapped the table. "I knew it. I was never sure the whole thing was for real or not, but how else did Caroline keep this place afloat? Look around. I bet you're trying to figure it out, too. There's not enough coming in with the cottages and snack bar to even pay the taxes. She had to have another source of money." The edge of Pearl's lip twitched up. "I think that's where your short fat guy came in. He came snooping around and I guess someone didn't like it." She leaned back in her chair. "We can split the treasure fifty-fifty. How does that sound?"

Hannah stood up and carried the empty mugs to her sink. "Seeing as I have the map, it doesn't sound very good for me. Would *you* take those odds?"

Pearl rubbed her chin and stared at Hannah. "Don't kid yourself, honey. You can't carry Caroline's lunch bucket in the bluffing department. You *need* my help."

Hannah placed both hands on the table and leaned inches away from Pearl's face. "I don't think so. The map is all I have to keep me from being the next one to get a knife in my back."

Pearl laughed. A deep evil laugh. "And what's going to protect your sister Ruby and her sweet little girl Olivia? Huh? Answer *that*."

Hannah felt her hands turn to ice. She reached down and gave another treat to Petunia but never took her eyes off Pearl's face. "I'll protect them. Just like I always have."

"You are a stupid girl, Hannah Holiday. Caroline would be so disappointed in you and your recklessness." She pushed herself out of the chair. "This isn't over. Not by a long shot. I've waited too long to lose this treasure now, to the likes of," she waved her hand, "you. I was patient waiting for Caroline to kick the bucket, but my well of patience is almost on empty. You better watch your back." She walked to the door. "Come on Petunia." She turned her head to look at Hannah one last time. "By the way, I need more towels in my cottage. Your rude employee, what's her name? Meg? She refused to give me extra towels for Petunia's baths."

The door slammed and Hannah sank into her chair. Nellie leaned against her, providing a bit of comfort. She stroked the soft fur until her hands stopped shaking. She wasn't sure if it was from fear or anger. Probably both.

Hannah looked around the small cottage that she now called home. "Okay, Great Aunt Caroline, I could use some help right about now."

Footsteps clumped on her porch, startling Hannah. Her heart raced. Was Caroline sending her help or was Pearl coming back to kill her?

"You look like you just saw a ghost," Jack said as he entered the cottage without knocking. "What's going on?"

Meg followed behind Jack. "Ready to hear our plan?"

"It has to be better than the last plan that was thrown in my face fifteen minutes ago." Hannah was skeptical that there wan an easy solution.

Meg and Jack looked at each other, puzzled by Hannah's frustrated tone.

Hannah summarized Pearl's proposition and looked expectantly at her two friends. "What do I do now? She basically threatened Ruby and Olivia if I don't hand over the map."

Jack rubbed his hands together and smiled. "I love a challenge. I'll take care of Pearl. Caroline always said Pearl *thinks* she's smarter than she is." He checked the time. "You and Meg should get over to the Pub and Pool Hall. Drop some hints about the map and your raffle plans. Believe me, word will spread like wildfire."

"What about Ruby and Olivia? They're sitting ducks in that little house."

"Tell her to stay here at your place. Nellie will protect them," Jack said. "Call her now. I'll wait until they get here. Then Pearl and I will have a good time. Maybe I'll even let her take me for a spin in that sporty red car of hers. One thing I know about Pearl is she eats up flattery like others eat up creamy delicious chocolate bon bons."

Chapter 13

Meg and Hannah drove to the Pub and Pool Hall. Meg insisted on driving her run-down, rattle-trap of a car. She said it would fit in with the local color better than Hannah's yuppie Volvo station wagon. Hannah didn't argue. She watched through the window as the houses of Hooks Harbor got farther apart and she tried to ignore the spring poking into her butt.

"When is Michael going to fix those lights?" Hannah asked when they finally bumped into the pothole-filled parking lot. "Isn't he getting tired of seeing *ub and Poo all*?"

"He *has* fixed it several times, but someone always climbs up on the roof and knocks the same lights out. I guess it's become the joke around the pool table. Michael's afraid that one of these times, whoever climbs up will be so drunk they'll fall off, break a leg, and sue him so he's leaving it as is."

Hannah laughed. "Then he'd have to change it to *u sue all.*"

"Not funny, Hannah." But Meg did let out a small chuckle. She patted Hannah's leg. "Ready to channel your inner Caroline and hit this place with both feet on the ground?"

"Sure, whatever that's supposed to mean. I'm not the new kid in town anymore."

"Yeah, right! You've only been here for what? Maybe four months? You'll be the new kid in town until your hair turns gray and you get some character wrinkles on your face."

Hannah slid out of Meg's car. "Looks busy tonight. I don't think I've been here on a Friday night before."

"Really? You're in for a treat. Friday night is when everyone spends a big chunk of their paycheck to get loud and rowdy and forget their problems. It's usually Michael's biggest night for bucks and trouble."

Hannah inhaled and exhaled. Noise drifted from the pub—music, yelling and a bit of loud indecipherable crashes. What was she walking into?

Too late to worry about that. She squared her shoulders and tossed her head back. She checked for cash in her jeans pocket and shoved it down as far as possible. No sense risking losing any money.

She felt Meg's fingers tighten on her arm and she nodded toward the door. "That guy walking inside looks like trouble with a capitol T."

Rocky, Hannah said to herself. Let the fun begin.

Michael nodded to Meg. His hands were full delivering drinks to his customers at the bar. With a tilt of his head, he motioned to a couple empty stools at the end of the bar. By the time they waded through the crowd, Michael had two beers sitting in front of the empty stools, waiting for them.

"Glad you two are here. Lots of new faces in the crowd. And from the chatter I'm hearing, the new faces are also unhappy," Michael said before he dashed away to satisfy other customers.

"How does your brother stand dealing with this stuff day after day?" Hannah asked Meg.

Meg took a long swallow of her beer. She wiped her mouth with the back of her hand. "Michael loves drama. He may sound like he's complaining but he thrives on this. Plus, the money's not too bad." She grinned. "Actually, he's a wealthy guy but don't let that get out. I've been sworn to secrecy."

A burst of arguing erupted by the pool table. Hannah elbowed Meg. "You were right on about trouble walking in. Looks to me like Pearl's clan isn't getting along too well." Hannah slid off the barstool before Meg could stop her and she marched toward the five men she remembered from Pearl's cottage.

Rocky saw her coming and gave her a toothy grin. "Hey Doll Face. I didn't think this joint was fancy enough for the likes of you. Nice to know you don't mind lowering your standards once in a while." He wiggled his eyebrows suggestively.

Hannah ignored his attempt at flirting with her. "And I didn't think it was scummy enough for the likes of you, Rocky. But here you are, and it makes me curious what you and your cronies are doing hanging out at the pool hall in Hooks Harbor."

Conversation near Hannah died down. She felt many eyes on her. She had to be careful.

"Just enjoying the scenery. And the women." Rocky snickered. "They aren't all as snooty as you, Ms. Hannah Holiday. As a matter of fact, I met a real nice dame staying in one of your cottages."

"Sherry Wolfe? The retired teacher? I wouldn't have pegged the two of you having anything in common. Or is she standing in as a mother figure? You know, someone to teach you some manners and refine you a bit?"

Rocky's eyes narrowed. "A school teacher? That's not what she told me." He scratched his head. "Can't believe anything you hear around this dopey town."

Meg finally managed to get Hannah's attention and whispered to her, "Challenge him to a game of pool. That'll ruffle his ego when you beat him."

"So, Rocky, I've got a proposition for you."

"Oh, I like the sound of that, Doll Face. I knew you'd eventually see the light."

"A game of pool. For a map if you win. Pearl already tried to bargain for it. And," she paused, "a one thousand dollar donation to the Hooks Harbor Library if *I* win." Hannah noticed Rocky's eyes darken. She leaned close enough to smell the beer on his breath. She whispered, "Yeah, you didn't expect her to go behind your back bargaining for the map, did you? You two were a tag team. Did she have you do all her dirty work for a cut? Huh?" Rocky's jaw muscles kicked into high gear, but for once he bit his tongue and kept quiet. Hannah handed him a pool stick. "You can break."

Hannah felt sweat drip down her side. It tickled but nothing was funny about the situation she'd put herself in. This map was all she had to smoke out the killer, and if she misjudged Rocky and lost the game, well, she couldn't even think about that option.

She saw Rocky quickly wipe sweat from his upper lip. Good, he was feeling the heat, too.

His break was powerful and the purple, solid four ball crashed into the side pocket. Rocky smiled and smirked at Hannah. "I've gotcha now Doll Face."

Hannah smiled. "Not on your life, Rocky." Her words threw him off enough that he just missed his next shot. He glared at Hannah.

Hannah walked around the table and called her shot. With each ball she sank, her confidence grew until she had one striped ball left. She missed.

Rocky's mouth twitched. "Such a shame. You were doing okay for a dame." He studied the table and sank four more solids. "I let you feel good about yourself for a few minutes, Doll Face. I can smell that treasure and it smells like a million bucks."

Rocky lined up his cue stick for another shot. A difficult one. Hannah noticed a slight shake. She smiled. He missed and left her setup for an easy shot to win.

"Tough break, Rocky." Hannah easily sank her last striped ball and the eight ball to win.

Rocky cursed under his breath. "You cheated."

Meg stood between the two players. "None of that trash talk. Lose like a man or get out." She glared at Rocky.

"Before you go," Hannah said, "I'll give you another chance to get the map you so covet. I'm raising money for the Hooks Harbor Library and I'll raffle it off at four tomorrow afternoon. Your one thousand dollar check will be the perfect start." She looked around the pool hall. "Spread the word. Let's get the whole town out for this event. I want to honor the memory of my Great Aunt Caroline with this gesture. And, who knows, maybe the treasure map will lead someone to a fortune."

The pub buzzed with chatter.

Rocky leaned toward Hannah, his stale breath hot on her cheek. "Think you're cute, don'tcha. You'll regret this, just like your cute little niece's dad and his sidekick."

Hannah's blood ran cold. "What did you say?"

Rocky's mouth twisted into a sneer. "I thought that might get your attention. Your sister always running away from Mr. Bigshot Lenny DiMarco. Want to rethink your plans with that map before someone else gets hurt?"

Hannah clenched her fists into tight balls. She would have loved to bury them in Rocky's face until her fear dissolved but she refused to give him the satisfaction of knowing he hit a nerve. "Not on your life, you low-life piece of scum."

Rocky shrugged. "Have it your way, but make sure you lock your doors good and tight, Doll Face." He laughed as he left the pub with the rest of his clan after he slapped the one thousand dollar check on the pool table.

Chapter 14

"That went well," Meg said after she and Hannah returned to their stools at the end of the counter.

"What's wrong, Hannah?" Michael asked.

Hannah stood up. Was it that obvious that she was worried? So much for a poker face today. "I need to go home and check on Ruby and Olivia."

"Stay here," Michael said. He motioned to one of his buddies. "Drive to Hannah's cottage and keep an eye on it until she gets home. Make sure no one goes in or out."

A simple nod, no words, and Michael's friend disappeared.

"Okay. Now we can get back to making our plans for tomorrow."

No sooner than those words were out of his mouth, the door opened and Jack entered. "Good, you're still here."

"Where's Pearl?" Hannah asked, her voice betraying deep concern. "Ruby and Olivia are alone at my cottage. Pearl and Rocky both threatened to use them to get the map."

Jack put his hand on Hannah's arm. "They're fine. The cottage is locked up tighter than a vault and Nellie is with them. Don't worry. Besides, Pearl dropped me off here on her way to town."

Michael had a pad of paper and jotted down information as fast as Meg dictated. Meg turned to Hannah. "Don't worry about tomorrow, we'll get the food all put together. I've got Caroline's recipes, which I doubt I'll even need, and I'll get up early to prepare the lobster rolls, clam chowder, and slaw here in Michael's kitchen. I can do it in my sleep if I have to."

With Hannah's worries calmed, Jack pulled Hannah to a corner table for two. "I got some information from Pearl."

Hannah was skeptical. "How do you know if you can believe anything she says?"

"Like I told you before, Pearl caves to flattery. She's always been like that, and I think she's interested in me."

"Oh? I didn't think she was your type. Too wild." With a twinkle in her eye, she added, "It must be that red convertible."

Jack shrugged. "Nope. She's not my type, but I did enjoy the ride. I know how to play her game to get what I want. She was always jealous of the close relationship Caroline and I had, and she thinks she can push in on that now that Caroline is gone. Pearl would get enormous satisfaction from thinking she won that competition."

"A game only she was playing, right?"

"Yeah, I suppose so. She always wanted to beat Caroline at something."

"Okay. It doesn't seem like it would be particularly satisfying to beat someone who's no longer walking the earth," Hannah said. "So what did you learn from her?"

Jack leaned back. "The short fat guy? Marco Russo. Caroline hired him to find Olivia's dad."

Hannah shot forward. "What? Why would she do that?"

"According to Pearl, she wanted whoever the dad was to pull his weight financially in Olivia's life. Caroline approached Pearl for a recommendation. You know, because of her ties with that shady crowd. The only problem was, once Caroline found out who he was, she understood why Ruby kept it a secret."

Hannah pulled her braid and chewed on the end. "But she opened a can of worms, didn't she?"

"Uh huh." Jack nodded. "She sure did, especially since she paid Marco with a copy of the map."

Hannah leaned back. "Something doesn't add up. How did Lenny get a copy of the map? Did Marco give it to him?"

"Pearl seems to think Marco shared the map with Lenny to get Lenny's help finding the treasure. Not exactly a match made in heaven."

"And Pearl told you all this because . . . ?" Hannah raised her eyebrows and waited for Jack's response.

He grinned. "Like I said, she's got a crush on me."

Hannah stood up. "Let's see if Meg and Michael are done with their planning. I'd really like to get home, check on Ruby and Olivia, and get a good night sleep before tomorrow arrives. With the way these last couple of days have gone, tomorrow will most likely be another doozy."

"Hannah?" Jack touched her arm, keeping her at the booth and away from the crowd. "Pearl is a conniving creature. One talent she always beat Caroline in was manipulating people to get her way. She's dangerous."

"Dangerous enough to have killed two people to get that buried treasure?"

"I think that's more than possible."

"Yeah, the thought crossed my mind, too. Pearl, together with her grandson Rocky. Do you think they're working together on this?"

Jack pursed his lips. "That's a tough call. My guess would be that Pearl wants it all for herself. She has always been the greedy type. But, Rocky is her grandson. I suppose if she could be sure none of it would go to her ex-husband, Tony, maybe she would work with Rocky."

"I suspect they're both dangerous, whether they work together or alone," Hannah said before joining Meg at the bar. "How's the plan coming?"

Meg slipped her notebook in her pocket. "Done. Everything's all set for tomorrow. Michael will get the word out. We'll start serving at noon and the raffle winner will be picked at four. How does that sound?" She looked at Hannah and Jack.

"Perfect," they both answered in unison.

"I'll offer beer at a discount for anyone buying a raffle ticket so that should open the floodgates," Michael told the others.

High fives went around the group. "Ready to head home?" Meg asked.

"You read my mind. I can't wait to slide under my covers and put this day behind me," Hannah replied as she followed Meg outside and slid into the back seat of Meg's car behind Jack.

The three rode in a comfortable silence. The car bounced along the uneven dirt road, throwing Hannah back and forth on the seat. One pothole bounced her so high her head hit the ceiling. "Ouch. Slow down Meg."

Hannah heard a loud bang and the car lurched sideways and suddenly stopped. Hannah groaned and climbed out to survey the damage. "I can't believe this happened." She slammed her hand on the side of the car.

"Don't worry. I'll have this fixed in just a few minutes," Meg told Hannah as she opened the trunk and lifted out the spare tire. "Uh oh. This isn't a good sign." They all stared at the flat spare.

Hannah had her phone out. "I'm calling Ruby to make sure she's okay."

Meg called her brother. "New plan," she announced after she hung up. "One of Michael's friends will pick us up and I'll deal with this problem tomorrow." She kicked the flat tire and mumbled something that was probably best left indecipherable.

"Ruby isn't answering. What should I do?" Hannah's eyes widened. Fear clenched her stomach. "I'm calling Cal to check on her. Something isn't right. I know her. Both Pearl and Rocky threatened to use her to get the map. Do you think they would hurt her? Or Olivia?"

Jack put his hand on Hannah's shoulder. "There's probably a logical explanation. Maybe she turned her phone off."

Hannah shook her head. "No. Her phone is her lifeline." She paced on the side of the road, letting her mind run away from her.

"If anything happens to them, I . . ." Her words trailed off into an unspoken world of fear.

A pickup truck stopped behind Meg's car. She waved. "Looks like Pete's going to be our chauffeur. He's quiet and a little rough around the edges but a genuine guy. Nothing underhanded about him."

They climbed in, Jack and Hannah in the back and Meg next to Pete up front. "Flat tire?" Pete asked.

"More like a blowout. This road is bad news on tires."

"Yup."

That was the extent of the conversation until Pete pulled up at Hannah's cottage next to Michael's other friend who had been keeping an eye on the comings and goings—or, hopefully, the lack thereof.

The other guy leaned out the window. "Haven't seen any activity. I'm heading home now."

"Thanks you two. Lobster rolls on the house for you both tomorrow," Hannah said.

Pete grinned. "Glad to help out Michael and Meg's friends. You take care now."

Meg hopped out too. "I'll crash at your house, Jack, seeing as I'll be needing a ride back to the pub tomorrow morning bright and early." They watched the two trucks back out. "That was the longest sentence I ever heard from his mouth, Hannah. I guess you made his day with the offer of a lobster roll."

Cal ran toward the threesome. "Something's wrong. No one is answering when I knock on Hannah's door."

Hannah dashed to her cottage, fumbling in her pocket for her keys. They crashed to the ground and Cal grabbed the key ring before Hannah could bend down. He got the door open in a flash.

"Ruby? Are you here?" Silence.

Nellie met Hannah with a wagging tail. The bedroom was empty. "Where did they go, Nellie?"

A piece of paper stuck out from under the coffee pot and caught Hannah's attention. She unfolded it. *Had to leave. Something isn't feeling right. I have to trust my instincts. Will be in touch. Love, Ruby.* "She must have left before Michael's friend even got here to watch the cottage."

"Where would she go?" Cal asked.

"That's the problem. I never know. She just disappears and all I can do is hope for the best. But this time is by far the most serious situation. Before, she would always be one step ahead of Lenny. Now his baggage caught up with her. And my fear is that it has gotten out of control." Hannah sank onto her couch. "What am I going to do now?" she asked no one in particular, her desperation clear in her voice.

Chapter 15

Hannah slept. Not well, between the tossing and turning, but at least it was something.

Jack knocked on her door early, after he dropped Meg off at the Pub and Pool Hall to start the food prep. He had a couple of day old cider donuts and, without any words between them, he got busy making fresh coffee in Hannah's kitchen.

Once the coffee started dripping, Jack broke the silence. "She'll call. You have to trust her instincts."

A big sigh escaped through Hannah's lips. "I know, but it isn't easy." She stared up at Jack. "Why didn't she tell me where she was going?"

"She was probably afraid there was a chance the wrong person would find the information."

"But how do I know she wasn't followed? Someone is out there that already killed two people, so what would stop them from killing her?"

Jack sat next to Hannah. "Well, she doesn't have the map. That's what this is all about. The map is here in Hooks Harbor as far as the killer knows. You are more of a target than Ruby is. Look at the positive side. You can focus on flushing out the bad guy without having her walk in the cross hairs."

"Nice try, Jack, but that doesn't make me feel one iota better. I'd much rather know exactly where the two of them are so I can keep them safe." Arguing outside made Hannah bolt from her chair. "Great. That sounds like Pearl and Sherry are at it again."

Once outside, Hannah couldn't help but laugh. What met her eyes was Petunia, dressed in a pink ballerina tutu. "You're going to give that poor pig a complex, Pearl. Why do you keep insisting on dressing her like she's your kid?"

"Thank you for taking my side, Hannah," Sherry said. "I just made the same point to your resident keeper of swine."

Pearl huffed and continued to her car. As she passed Hannah, she said under her breath, "I can't believe what you are planning to do today. That treasure was promised to *me* and I intend to find it."

Hannah grabbed Pearl's arm. "Who promised it to you?"

"Are you daft? I explained it all to Jack last night. Caroline promised when I helped her find that scummy investigator, Marco Russo. But your aunt," Pearl took out a cigarette, "paid that scumball with a copy of the treasure map, too. And, from what I can gather, he shared it with your niece's dad. The two of them tried to sneak into town, but nothing Marco ever does is off the radar of my grandson."

Pearl lit her cigarette and inhaled deeply, tilted her head backwards, and sighed. "I can't believe I thought I could ever give this up."

Hannah moved upwind of Pearl. "And Rocky stayed with you the night Lenny was killed. I saw him outside wandering around. He gave me some lame excuse that he was looking for Petunia." Hannah leaned right against Pearl. "You know what I think? He let Petunia roam around so he could use her as an excuse to stick his nose where it didn't belong."

Pearl moved back a pace.

"Or," Hannah moved close again. "Or he found Lenny sneaking around the snack bar and stabbed him." Hannah poked Pearl when she said the word stabbed.

Pearl jumped and a small eeek escaped along with her cigarette smoke. "How *dare* you accuse my Rocky of anything of the sort? He's much too sensitive to even look at a spot of blood."

"Yeah, right. Rocky had to get Lenny out of the way so there was one less person to fight over the treasure with."

Hannah noticed Sherry pretending not to stare at Pearl. With a sly grin she approached. "I couldn't help but overhear your conversation. I saw something the first day I arrived."

"I'm sure you did," Pearl said. "You're always sneaking around, poking your nose in other people's business. My Rocky told me you've been hanging around at the pub, asking questions."

Sherry took a step back. "Well, that's how you find out information. I was thinking of moving to this town, and the local watering hole is the perfect spot to find out the flavor of the area. And, I might add, it's not to my liking so far."

Jack touched Sherry's arm, trying to distract her and get her back to her original thoughts. "What did you see on Wednesday, the day you arrived?"

"Well, I'm a very observant person, but sometimes what you see doesn't take on meaning until later. You know what I mean? And now with these two murders," she paused and a shudder went through her body, "I recognized the photos of the two men on the news." She looked from Jack to Hannah to Pearl. "I saw them. The good looking one picked up the short guy in town."

"Where did they go?" Hannah asked. "This could be important information. Did you tell Officer Larson when she questioned everyone?"

"Oh, I didn't think about it then. Like I said, it didn't take on any meaning until now, when I heard you two arguing. I said to myself, Sherry, those two poor men knew each other. These murders must be connected."

Pearl dropped her cigarette butt and ground it into the sand. "Of course they're connected. That's no news to me." She pulled on Petunia's leash and continued to her car.

"Well, isn't she a grouchy old lady," Sherry observed. "I don't know what she has against *me*. There's something else that's been sort of bothering me." She looked at Hannah and Jack. "You know how I like to walk on the beach? I'm a very routine kind of gal."

Jack covered a choke by pretending he was coughing.

"Did you see something, Sherry? On the beach?" Hannah asked, hoping this might lead to some useful information. Maybe even an explanation as to how Lenny's shirt ended up buried in the sand.

"As a matter of fact, I did see something. But again, who knows if it's relevant to these terrible murders." She swiveled her head and gazed at the view. "I think the ocean holds a lot of secrets, don't you?" She turned her focus back to Hannah.

"Yes, but the ocean isn't about to blab those secrets, is it? What did *you* see when you were walking on the beach?" Hannah was getting impatient and started to think Sherry only wanted some attention. She was stuck at the cottage until Officer Larson said she could leave. She didn't know anyone. She seemed to have a bit of a crush on Jack. Was this her way to make them spend time with her?

"I saw tracks in the sand. Beyond that rocky outcrop where the waves don't wash them away." Sherry's words startled Hannah back to the moment.

"What kind of tracks?"

"Well, I put my foot into one and it was several sizes bigger. So, maybe a man's footprint? And there were cracker wrappers too. Half buried under one of the footprints." She stuck her hand in her pocket. "This is what I found. It's probably nothing, but it does make you wonder, doesn't it?"

"Wonder what?" Hannah asked. Her nerves where on edge after recognizing the peanut butter cracker wrappers. The same thing she found near Lenny's buried shirt.

"I wonder how that cute guy survived the boating accident only to get stabbed in the back under your snack bar." Sherry's eyes wandered to the murder scene. A tremor went through her body. "What was Pearl talking about when she mentioned a treasure map? That certainly sounds interesting, although a bit farfetched." She raised her eyebrows.

Jack, who had been standing quietly during the conversation, finally spoke up. "Listen, anyone interested in some coffee? I'd be happy to make some."

"Jack, that sounds perfect. You read my mind. I knew you were a sensitive type," Sherry gushed.

Hannah added, "Sorry, I'll have to pass. I should get over to the Pub and Pool Hall and help Meg. It will distract me from worrying about Ruby, too."

"Your sister?" Sherry asked. "Is everything all right with her and that darling little girl? She left in a bit of a hurry last night. And it looked like a car followed her out of the parking lot."

"What time?"

"Well, I'm not sure. I went outside to listen to the waves. It's such a relaxing sound, don't you think? Anyway, I heard your door slam, and when I turned around, your sister was practically running to her car." Sherry pointed to the parking lot. "I thought she was rushing home to put her daughter to bed. You know, mothers these days don't keep to a rigid schedule like I always did."

"And the car that followed her? What did it look like?" Hannah asked, not really wanting to know the answer if it was what she suspected.

"A big, dark Cadillac."

Chapter 16

Cal arrived with a truck full of lumber for more picnic tables. He parked his truck and carried a bag toward Hannah. "Breakfast?" he asked cheerfully, holding the brown paper bag in her direction.

"I've lost my appetite."

"What's wrong?" Cal put his hand on Hannah's waist and guided her to her cottage.

Absentmindedly, Hannah opened Cal's offering and took out a breakfast burrito. She took a bite. And another. Cal poured her a mug of coffee and sat down at the table with her.

"Where's everyone else? It's kind of quiet around here."

"Jack is entertaining Sherry at his house. Making her coffee I think. Sherry's quite delighted. Meg's at the Pub and Pool Hall getting food ready for my opening that's *not* happening here. Ruby and Olivia—"

Hannah's head fell onto her arms resting on the table. Her shoulders shook as she sobbed. Her worry for Ruby and Olivia overwhelmed her power to even finish her thought.

Hannah's phone buzzed. She looked at it, grabbed it, and paced around her room.

"Ruby. Where are you?" Hannah asked almost hysterically. "Okay, call me in an hour."

"Is she all right?" Cal asked, his brow furrowed.

Hannah nodded. "For now. She's staying with a friend. She wouldn't tell me where, but she'll keep checking in. I don't like it, but I wouldn't even know where to start looking for her."

A knock interrupted their conversation. Cal went to the door to see who was there.

"Um. I guess we're ready to check out but no one was in the office," Aaron Masterson said a bit sheepishly. "Sorry to bother you."

"No bother Aaron," Hannah said as she walked to her office.

"Don't leave without me when you head over to the pub," Cal called over his shoulder as he headed to his truck to unload the lumber.

Hannah opened the office door for Aaron. "Where's your wife?"

"She's finishing the packing. I'll drop the key off on our way to the car. Is that okay?" Aaron shifted his weight from one foot to the other.

"Have a seat. Is everything all right?" Hannah pulled a chair closer to her desk for him.

Aaron looked around the room, everywhere but at Hannah. "Not really," he finally blurted out. "That woman staying in one of the cottages has been awfully nosy."

"Which one?"

"Not the teacher. She's been respectful of our privacy. The other one. With purple hair and a pig." Aaron paused. "I don't want to cause trouble. Your cottage is amazing, and listening to the ocean has been very peaceful. We'd love to come back sometime."

Hannah was pretty sure he didn't mean what he just said but was trying to make her feel better. "I'd love to have you back." Hannah rested her arms on her desk and leaned over toward Aaron. "What happened with Pearl? She was an old friend of my Great Aunt Caroline, who I inherited the cottages from, and she kind of showed up out of the blue. I never met her before. What did she do?"

"We caught her snooping around our cottage after we went out for a walk. She said she went into the wrong cottage by accident but, come on, it was locked. Somehow she broke in."

Hannah nodded. "Did she take anything?"

"No. But she was down on her hands and knees rummaging around in the closet when we walked in."

"Whatever for?"

Aaron flicked his wrist. "She laughed it off and mumbled something about her secret compartment." He twirled his finger in a circle next to the side of his head. "I think she must have a few screws loose. Probably harmless but Laura's been a nervous wreck ever since."

"I'm sorry about that. I wish you had told me sooner so I could have had a word with her."

"There's more," Aaron continued.

Hannah felt her stomach drop. What was Pearl up to? Searching for the buried treasure one cottage at a time? Is that what spooked Ruby to leave in such a hurry?

Aaron's words broke through her thoughts when she heard him say *Rocky.*

"What?"

"That kid Rocky. Every night we'd see him walking around. He'd pace off carefully, dig a hole, cover it, and repeat the whole process in a different direction. What's he looking for? A body?" Aaron stood up. "We love everything about this place except your other guests. My advice if you want to make a go of it here—vet everyone better."

Hannah was stunned. Pearl and Rocky were searching for the treasure. Right under her nose. How did she miss it?

She held Aaron's arm. "Let me make it up to you. What you've just told me is completely unacceptable. Spend the rest of your week, no charge. Pearl is a bit, um, odd, but she's not dangerous."

"I don't know," Aaron waffled. "Laura's really spooked. And those two murders? One right here under your snack bar? A bit much for us. We wanted peace and quiet by the ocean, and it would have been perfect without all those distractions." Aaron stared at Hannah. "How can you be sure she's not dangerous?"

Hannah chose to ignore the last question. "Talk to Laura. I'll get the problem sorted out. Pearl's grandson isn't even supposed to be staying here. And Sherry Wolfe? Has she bothered you?"

"Oh no. She told us about some nice trails along the beach and even brought us a basket of goodies when she found out we're newlyweds. An odd assortment of snacks but the gesture was appreciated." Aaron turned to leave. "I'll talk to Laura but I'm pretty sure her mind is made up."

Hannah's heart went out to this young man. He had an awful experience in her cottage when it should have been a romantic honeymoon getaway.

The office door opened and an icy chill made Hannah shiver.

"Hello, Mr. Masterson, not thinking of checking out all ready, are you?" Officer Pam Larson blocked the doorway with a half grin on her face. "You need to stay in town at least through the weekend." Pam flung her arm toward the ocean. "But who would want to leave this beautiful paradise?"

Aaron looked from Pam to Hannah. "I'll explain the situation to Laura. And thanks for the offer. It looks like we will take you up on it, after all." His glum face betrayed his real feelings about the situation as he walked passed Pam.

Pam pulled the door closed. "What's up with the newlyweds? I should imagine he and his wife would be loving it here—ocean, beaches, romantic walks under the stars."

"Yeah, well," Hannah motioned for Pam to have the seat recently vacated by Aaron, "he walked in on Pearl Martini in his cottage. Searching for, what she called, her secret compartment, in his closet."

Pam entwined her fingers and rested her hands on her lap. "Ah, yes. Searching for the buried treasure in a closet?" Pam mocked Hannah's comment. "I suppose next you'll tell me she's been digging holes all over the place."

Hannah leaned toward Pam. "As a matter of fact, her grandson, Rocky, has been doing just that, according to Aaron. His wife is spooked and they wanted to check out early."

"Oh, Hannah. You certainly didn't inherit Caroline's shrewdness. Don't you see what he's doing?"

Hannah shrugged.

"Did you offer him free lodging?"

Hannah nodded. She slapped her forehead. "Are you serious? He made that story up about Pearl breaking into his cottage?"

Pam put her hands behind her head and relaxed back in the chair. "I've seen everything, and his story is a bit farfetched. Let's suppose there is a buried treasure, it wouldn't be in a closet. And, even *you* would have noticed holes all over the place. I doubt that grandson, with an IQ of a pea, would know how to cover his tracks very well."

Pam was right. Hannah had to toughen up. If she had any chance of making this place a success, she couldn't fall for every sob story that hit her ears.

"I hear you've moved your grand opening to the Pub and Pool Hall," Pam said. "I'm sorry you had to do that but it may turn out to be a brilliant strategy."

Hannah rolled her eyes. "How do you figure that?"

"You're an outsider." Pam cocked her brows up. "That's the reality of your situation until you've been in this town for a long time. Teaming up with Michael gives you legitimacy in the eyes of the townies. As long as your food delivers, and with Meg handling that you don't have to worry, you'll be able to make a smooth transition to your snack bar when it finally does open."

Hannah nodded but she was wary. Pam wasn't usually friendly toward her, but Hannah hadn't figured out Pam's angle yet. There had to be an angle.

"I want to see that map."

That's the angle, Hannah thought. "I don't have it."

Pam stood up. "Does it exist?"

"Several versions exist."

"Don't be cute. Even though I don't believe there is a buried treasure, I do believe the *idea* of a buried treasure is connected to the two murders. And," she pierced Hannah with a stare, "I'm positive it's connected to your sister's disappearance."

The air rushed from Hannah's lungs. "You know about that?"

"Of course I do. Everything reaches these." Pam wiggled her ears with her thumb and first finger. "And I know where she is. She's safe. For now. But she's in danger. You too, for that matter. It doesn't matter if *I* think there actually is a buried treasure, someone, or multiple *someones*, believe it's real. That's why I want all your guests staying put through the weekend."

"Even Sherry Wolfe and Aaron and Laura Masterson? You think they could be involved with the murders?"

"Listen, Hannah. I'm not ruling anyone out. Not even you or your sister. We're keeping a close eye on her, especially after she ran off last night. And that little stunt Aaron Masterson just pulled with you? Was he trying to put the spotlight on someone else?"

Chapter 17

Hannah stayed in her chair after Pam left. A wave of incompetence surged through every bone, making her feel like Pam just put her through a blender and poured her on the ground. And probably stirred up the mess with the toe of her shoe. Then buried it all in one of the holes that Aaron talked about.

She sighed. At least the police were keeping tabs on Ruby and Olivia. She wasn't happy with the *reason* for the monitoring, but at least it would keep her sister and niece safe.

Before Hannah could get up from her desk and head to the Pub and Pool Hall, Cal walked into the office. "That bad, huh?"

"Every time Pam talks to me, I doubt my ability to be running this business. What was Great Aunt Caroline thinking leaving it to me? No experience. No confidence. And pretty soon, no money." Hannah rested her head on one hand.

"Aren't *you* the optimist today," Cal teased. "Don't forget what it says on my boat—*Seas the Day*. Are you ready?"

She shook her head. "Not really. I don't know where to start. Both Ruby and I are on Pam's suspect list, along with Pearl, Sherry, Aaron, and Laura. And, most definitely, Rocky." She looked at Cal. "I know I didn't kill anyone, but the others? What do you think?"

Cal's eyes wrinkled at the corners. "Probably Ruby. You know what a violent person *she* is." He motioned Hannah to follow him. "Let's sit outside on one of your new picnic tables and listen to the surf. That always helps clear the mind. I'm a firm believer that if you're out in nature, you *will* feel better. If the wind doesn't blow it away, the sun will cook it out of you."

Hannah followed Cal outside. With each step, she did feel a bit better. Looking at his backside didn't hurt. She giggled to herself. He turned and pointed at Hannah. "I caught you feeling better already. Let's make a plan on how to attack this problem."

They sat facing the ocean. The waves, with their never ending rush in and out, crashing on the sand, actually gave Hannah strength. The ocean never gave up and she wouldn't either.

Cal nudged her with his elbow after Hannah's fidgeting calmed down. "Good. I can hear your gears working. What have you come up with?"

"The key is the map. Even Pam admitted that whoever the murderer is believes it's real. I suppose that makes sense. Everyone wants to think they will find that pot at the end of a rainbow." She turned toward Cal. "Do *you* think it's real?"

"Me? Will that mean I'm a suspect?"

She jabbed him in the side. "No. I was only thinking maybe we should be looking for the treasure."

"Ninety nine percent of me doesn't believe it's real. But who knows for sure? Caroline was full of tricks so there could be something to it."

"Good. That's what I was hoping you would say. How about we create a buried treasure for someone to find?" She stood up and faced her snack bar. The yellow police tape was gone. "I know the perfect spot."

"The perfect spot for what?" Jack asked as he joined Hannah and Cal.

"What happened to Sherry? You managed to ditch her without a scene?" Hannah teased.

Jack shrugged. "She said she had someplace to be. I wasn't about to argue. She did ask a lot of questions about the buried treasure. It's funny how people latch onto a crazy idea like that." He sat at the picnic table with Hannah and Cal. "Fill me in. I can smell some plot hatching around here."

"I've decided it's time to bury a treasure," Hannah said as she chewed on the end of her braid. "Something, but I don't know what."

"You're a genius." Jack leaned close to Hannah until their shoulders touched. "I've got an old lock box that's kind of rusty on the corners. How about filling it with sand, shells, and sea glass? It will be a treasure chest of ocean valuables!"

Hannah put her hand out, palm up, for a high five. "You're the genius, Jack. Maybe we should throw in some sand dollars too, for the irony." Her words stumbled over each other in her excitement.

Jack slapped Hannah's palm. "I'll raid my beach collections and fill up the box nice and pretty." Jack was already on his feet and heading to his house. "Be right back with the box and the map."

Cal chuckled as he watched Hannah and Jack scheme. "I know my part in the plan," he said as he walked toward the snack bar. He was on his hands and knees looking under the snack bar by the time Hannah joined him. "Hiding the treasure under here will only work if it looks like I'm working on this last beam. Otherwise, all the nosy people around here will be suspicious."

They walked to his truck. "Somehow, I need to dig a deep hole, get the box in and make it look like it's been there all along, then slide the last beam in place."

"But you need to leave a big enough opening for someone to still be able to crawl in and find the treasure." Hannah stood with her hands on her hips watching Cal.

Cal pursed his lips. "How will this lead to the murderer, though? With the map being raffled off, anyone in town could search for it."

"True, but do you think anyone else in town would have killed Marco and Lenny? No one even knew them. I think the killer will keep an eye on whoever wins the map."

"I'm going to start working. You'll need to distract anyone who comes around." Cal got his shovel and started digging a trench where the last beam needed to go. Hannah busied herself, setting up the new picnic tables with umbrellas.

Aaron and Laura strolled by with a blanket and picnic basket. "It's kind of quiet around here today," Aaron said to Hannah as he looked around at the mostly deserted parking lot.

"I imagine most people will be at the Pub and Pool Hall."

"What's happening there?"

Hannah slid the last umbrella into its stand. "Today was *supposed* to be the grand opening for my snack bar but, well, I couldn't have it here." She grimaced. "For obvious reasons. So, the Pub and Pool Hall is the new location. And I'm not sure if you heard about the raffle?"

Laura's eyes lit up. "What kind of raffle? I love raffles."

"My Great Aunt Caroline left me a map for a buried treasure." Hannah watched a quick look pass between Aaron and Laura. "I'm raffling it off this afternoon. All the money will be donated to the Hooks Harbor Library."

"You're kidding!" Laura almost shouted. "My dad was always on the lookout for that kind of thing." She looked at Aaron and grinned. "He was sort of like the original treasure hunter. His friends always made fun of him but I still have all his notes on his research. That's sort of why we ended up here. He heard rumors about a treasure but died before he could follow up on the leads." Laura's eyes filled with tears and she looked away from Hannah.

Hannah's heart quickened. She hated to admit it, but Pam read those two to a T. Did Laura just spill the beans on something she should have kept secret? Maybe they weren't even on their honeymoon. Hannah made a mental note to look into that detail.

"Well, that does it then," Laura said with excitement, a tremble still clear in her voice. "We hadn't decided what we were going to do today, but the Pub and Pool Hall sounds like the place to be." Laura pulled Aaron toward their car. He kept glancing back at Hannah, making the hairs on her neck stand up.

Jack parked next to Cal's truck. He slid out and looked around quickly. "Is the coast clear?"

Hannah nodded. "Aaron and Laura just left. Sherry hasn't come back, and Pearl is gone, too." She popped the trunk of Jack's car. "This is perfect. Some rust, some dents, a lot of scratches in the enamel."

Jack smiled. "I added a few dents with a hammer. Glad you approve of that touch." He opened the lid to expose the treasure inside.

Hannah's eyes widened. "Where did you find all this beautiful glass? It sparkles in the sunshine." She dug her fingers in the box and sifted through blue and green sea glass mixed with smooth rocks, sand, shells, and a few sand dollars. A slight scent of salty ocean drifted to her nose.

"Caroline and I always gathered something when we walked the beach." Jack looked at the treasure, his thoughts lost in long ago adventures. "This comes from fifty plus years of collections. I suppose it's fitting to donate it to this cause even though I'm sad to part with the memories. If it flushes out a killer, Caroline would say I put it to good use." Jack picked up one piece of green glass and tucked it into his pocket before he gently closed the box and locked it. "Here." He handed the key to Hannah. "This should go with the map."

She nodded vigorously. "Nice touch. Makes the map more real."

Jack grinned. "The map *is* real now. We have to make sure it leads to the snack bar."

Cal pushed his wheelbarrow to the back of Jack's car. "I'll slide this under my tarp and get it into place. The hole is ready for the buried treasure." He slid the treasure box into the wheelbarrow and it landed with a dull thump. "This is turning into an exciting adventure."

"Come to my cottage after you get it buried," Hannah said. "We'll check the map and make sure it will lead someone to the right spot."

Jack followed Hannah inside. He opened the map she found several months earlier after she moved in and cleaned out her great aunt's belongings. "I've been studying this map and I think we were right when we first looked at it." Jack pointed to an X. "This certainly could be under the snack bar. And with Lenny getting stabbed in that spot, people will think he was hot on the trail of the treasure. I'm confident that our buried treasure will be discovered."

Hannah's phone rang just as Cal entered and she answered before the second ring. "Ruby?"

The blood in Hannah's veins ran cold. It was not Ruby's voice that answered. "Sorry, she can't come to the phone right now, dear."

"Pearl, put Ruby on," Hannah demanded.

"Hold your horses, dear. There's plenty of time for you to talk to your sister after you listen to what I need."

"The map?"

Pearl laughed a deep belly laugh. "Oh, Hannah. Again, you disappoint me. The Hooks Harbor folks can beat themselves to death over that silly map. No, I want Caroline's property in exchange for your sister and your adorable niece. Olivia, right? Doesn't that sound like a fair trade?"

The phone slipped from Hannah's fingers. Cal caught her as her legs buckled and he helped her to the couch. "What is it?" he asked, panic in his eyes.

Jack picked up the phone. "Pearl? Are you still there?"

"Yes, love," her voice, on speaker phone, filled the room. "What was that horrible crash? Is Hannah all right? She can't fall apart now or who knows what will happen to Ruby." The phone went dead.

Chapter 18

"She's bluffing," Jack said. "She won't hurt Ruby or Olivia. The last thing Pearl wants is to end up in jail where she would have to share a cell with someone. She doesn't share well."

"I know you're trying to make me feel better but it's not working," Hannah said, her elbows on her knees and her head resting on her hands. "Desperate people aren't predictable. Pearl showed up with an agenda and her cute pot belly pig as a distraction. I completely overlooked the possibility of another plan. The map was her way to connect with Great Aunt Caroline, or a sideshow to keep her grandson occupied. I never suspected she was after Great Aunt Caroline's property."

"*Your* property," Cal corrected. "It's yours now, Hannah, and Pearl's not going to take it away."

Jack was at the door. "I'm going to find Pam and make sure she's right on this. Pearl won't get far."

"Pam already told me someone was keeping an eye on Ruby and Olivia. Pam screwed up and somehow Pearl got by." Hannah's voice betrayed her fear.

"Don't count on it. Pam probably knows exactly what's going on," Jack said, trying to reassure Hannah before he left.

Hannah pushed a stray lock of hair behind her ear. "Jack has way more confidence in his daughter than I do. At the moment."

"At least he's on it. Let's get over to the Pub and Pool Hall. You have a grand opening to attend. This will be your chance to woo everyone in town with your beautiful smile, Meg's delicious lobster rolls, Caroline's clam chowder, and a buried treasure."

"Is the treasure buried under the snack bar?"

"Uh huh. And the last beam is in place, too. I didn't want to make it too easy for someone to squeeze under, but it's possible. A tight fit, and not for anyone with claustrophobia."

"I'll go lock everything up good and tight and grab the map. Be right back."

Hannah found an old envelope from a box full of Caroline's papers that she had saved. She slid the map and key inside, licked it, and pressed it until the glue stuck. She scrunched it, dropped it on the floor, and stepped on it a couple of times to dirty it up.

"This will have to do. Sorry Nellie. You'll have to stay here and guard everything. No dogs allowed in the pub." She slammed and locked the door, double checked to be sure it was secure, and joined Cal in his truck.

They bumped down the dirt road and passed Meg's car which was still stranded on the side of the road with its blown out tire. Cars spilled out of the Pub and Pool Hall parking lot, filling every possible spot.

Cal swerved between two small cars, his truck only inches from each car.

"How will we get out?" Hannah asked.

Cal slid the back window open and extended his hand. "Ladies first."

Hannah looked at Cal, then the rectangle of open window. "Are you serious?"

He grinned. "Yup. You'll have an easier time fitting through than I will. I locked myself out once and had to force the window open to get in. It was a tight fit."

"Head first or feet first?"

"Never mind. I'll go first so I can catch you when you push yourself through."

Hannah liked the sound of that. She didn't mind one bit falling into Cal's arms, even if it was in such an unromantic situation.

"What are you smiling about?" Cal grinned at Hannah.

"I can't wait to see how you do this. The window doesn't look big enough. I might have to give you a shove."

Cal put his arms and head through the window and wiggled his chest through. With a kick off the seat, the rest of his body slid through like a seal in the water. He turned toward the window and smiled at Hannah. "Your turn."

Hannah tucked her envelope with the map and key into the waistband of her jeans. She copied Cal's technique, and as her body started to fall toward the bed of the truck, his strong arms caught her and pulled her the rest of the way through. He slid the window shut and jumped off the bed of his truck. "That wasn't too bad. Maybe by the time we come back, one of these other cars will be gone and we won't have to go through the window again."

Hannah looked at the two cars on either side of Cal's truck. Fortunately, only one side of each car was blocked in by his truck so the door on the far side could still be opened and *they* wouldn't have to climb in through their trunk.

Country music blared from speakers on the roof. "Michael went all out for this event," Cal noted. "He even fixed the lights in his sign."

With his hand on the small of Hannah's back, Cal guided her to the door of the pub. The closer they got, the louder the mix of music, talking, and the crack of pool balls sounded. The scent of clam chowder drifted out the door making Hannah's mouth water.

Moving from the bright sunshine to the dim lighting inside the pub took her eyes several seconds to adjust. The crowd inside made her pause with anxiety but she pushed through and took another step forward. Someone walked by and bumped into her, knocking her against Cal. "Hey Doll Face, I gave up on you showing up for your own party. Grub's decent."

"Rocky. Where's your Nana? Is she coming too?" Hannah decided a bit of civility toward Rocky might get her the information she needed to find Ruby.

"Naw. She said she had something to do and I'm supposed to buy the raffle tickets for the map." He winked at Hannah. "All of them."

Hannah's right eyebrow shot up. "How are you going to manage that?"

Rocky pulled out a wad of bills. "Money talks, right Doll Face? I'm planning to offer to buy any raffle ticket for twenty bucks. Smart, huh?"

"Do you have any idea what the buried treasure is?" Hannah was intrigued with Rocky's strategy and extremely curious why he was willing to shell out so much money for something that might or might not even exist.

"Ha, nice try Doll Face. Lenny said you'd be asking a lot of questions. He was convinced that old lady Caroline buried something valuable. Maybe leaving a nice surprise for you or your sister."

Hannah pulled away from Cal, nodding for him to help Meg with the food. She inched closer to Rocky, knowing flattery was his drug in a conversation. "You certainly are a sharp planner, Rocky. Your nana must be pleased with your plan."

He waved that comment off with a quick flick of his wrist. "Nana doesn't have a clue. She's off chasing your sister, but that's not where the dough is." He tapped the side of his head with his finger. "I've got it all figgered out. She doesn't know I was pumping poor Lenny for information."

"Clever," Hannah gushed. "When did you last see Lenny? Alive?"

Rocky's eyes darkened. "What are you thinking, Doll Face. I didn't kill that creep."

Hannah gently placed her hand on his arm, cringing inside but keeping her face soft and friendly. "Of course not. I'm only trying to get the timeline straight."

"Oh, yeah, the timeline. Well, let me think. I followed your sister to a house and went in after she left. Lenny and that real slime ball, Marco, were having an argument when I walked in. No knocking, I just barged in and surprised them. Smart, huh? Caught 'em off guard."

Hannah nodded. "Very smart. You knew Marco?" Hannah had managed to slowly maneuver Rocky to a corner away from the crowd. She loved pumping him for information and figured no one gave him the attention he craved. In her mind, Hannah likened him to a needy puppy; eager to please in exchange for a coveted pat on his shaggy head.

"Sure. Nana used him for all sorts of stuff. Not anything I can share with you, though."

"What about Lenny? How well did you know him?"

Rocky's eyes brightened. "That's the funniest part. That old lady friend of Nana's, Caroline? She needed help finding someone. Some relative or something like that. Anyway, the guy she was looking for? Lenny? Turns out he was Marco's cousin or second cousin or at least somehow related. Caroline paid a bundle to Nana for what turned out to be a five minute job."

Lights were flashing in Hannah's head. All the connections were beginning to make sense. Lenny followed Ruby right to the buried treasure location. That must have been a plus for him and his sleaze-ball cousin. The rest of the mob followed Marco and Lenny.

"How about I buy you a beer, Rocky?" She already had her hand up to get Michael's attention and she pulled a couple of chairs to a small round table for herself and Rocky. "Make yourself comfy. I'll be right back."

Rocky had a wide, self-satisfied smile on his face. "I knew you'd come around, Doll Face. No one can resist Rocky's charm."

Hannah patted his shoulder as she moved to the bar to get the beer. Cal whispered, "What's going on? Are you ditching me for that mobster?"

"Seriously, Cal? I'm playing to his ego to loosen his tongue. And boy oh boy, does he love to talk."

Hannah set a beer in front of Rocky. "So, where were we?" She leaned across the small table and whispered close to Rocky's ear, "Do you think Lenny killed Marco? Weren't they out on that boat together?"

"I don't know about that. I always suspected Lenny was working with someone else and he just threw the body overboard."

"Who would that be?"

"Your sister? Ya know, find the treasure and split it two ways? She did meet him to cook up something. Cut *you* right out." He winked at Hannah. "You and me? We could beat her to it if we team up. Whaddya think? You still got the map?"

Hannah sat back so fast the front legs of her chair lifted off the floor. Was he playing her for a fool instead of her finding out useful information? Was he smarter than she gave him credit for?

Hannah felt an arm around her shoulder. She looked up to see Cal staring at Rocky, sending a signal not to mess with her. Cal squeezed her shoulder. "Everything all right here?"

"Sure thing, dude." Rocky stood up. "Think about it, Doll Face. I'm not going anywhere. At least not till I've got that map." He patted his pocket full of money and winked at Hannah.

Chapter 19

"What was that all about?" Cal asked as he slid onto the seat vacated by Rocky. "You can close your mouth now," he teased as he gently pinched Hannah's lips together.

"I wish I knew the answer to your question. Just when I think I have the upper hand, they manage to twist the conversation around to make me feel like a complete and total incompetent fool."

"They?" Cal twisted his head around in the direction where Rocky disappeared. "I thought you were talking to only one person. Or," he smirked, "maybe just half a person."

"*They* meaning Pearl, and now Rocky. He acts like such a doofus, but he led me right down the path to where he wanted me."

Cal's brow furrowed. "I'm not liking the sound of where that path is taking you."

"The path of doubting my own sister and trying to manipulate me to help him find the buried treasure."

"Oh, that's all." Cal wiped his brow of pretend sweat. "I thought it was some romantic path, *Doll Face*."

Hannah slapped Cal's arm. "Not funny, Mister." She leaned closer to Cal. "And listen to this, he's planning to buy the raffle tickets from everyone so he has all of them. I want that money to go to the library."

"How about instead of a raffle, you sell the map to the highest bidder? Auction it off. I'll get a bunch of guys to bid the price up so Rocky has to spend all his money and the library gets it. I'll even get a spicy rumor started about what the treasure might be. Maybe . . . gold coins or jewelry or an antique silver tea set."

"No, we can't change the rules at this point. According to Michael, raffle tickets are selling like hot cakes. We might still be able to beat him at his own game, though. Get the rumor mill working about the treasure and that should make it harder for Rocky to buy up the tickets. Maybe there really is a valuable buried treasure out there."

"Ha, didn't you see the same thing I saw?" Cal checked around him to the left and right. "Worthless baubles."

"Pearl wants the property. Maybe she knows something we haven't figured out yet."

Cal stood up. "Possible, but I'm leaning more toward what Meg and Jack said about it being a hoax. They were both close to Caroline. If they suspected something, don't you think this whole search fiasco would have happened years ago? Why now?"

"Good point. With Great Aunt Caroline out of the way, Pearl figures she can manipulate me or scare me to death by kidnapping Ruby. It's working, too."

Cal held Hannah's shoulders. "Listen. Ruby is worth nothing to Pearl if she hurts her. She wants a trade and she's counting on you blinking first. I'll get the buzz started about the map and see what kind of scum we flush out of the woodwork." He gazed into Hannah's eyes. "Okay?"

She nodded.

Hannah finally pushed her way through the crowd to check with Meg and find out how the lobster rolls and clam chowder were selling.

"Fantastic," Meg said as she filled three more bowls. "I hope we don't run out. This is whetting everyone's appetite for when the snack bar is finally open for business."

Hannah was relieved with that good news. "Cal got the last beam in place, so as soon as the inspector comes back we'll be able to open."

Meg pushed a bowl of chowder into Hannah's hand. "You need to eat something. Circulate, say hello to everyone. And, Hannah? Wipe that worried look off your face. Channel Caroline. Be friendly, tough, and pushy."

Hannah turned around and almost dumped her bowl of chowder down the front of Sherry's neatly ironed, button down shirt. "So sorry."

Sherry stepped to one side. "You're just the person I've been looking for. I'm curious about the buried treasure map that Jack told me about. It does make for an interesting story for this little town."

Hannah tried to sip her chowder without spilling any down the front of her own shirt, never mind on someone else. It didn't go well. "It's something I found when I was sorting through my great aunt's belongings. You know, after I inherited the property."

Sherry touched Hannah's arm, jostling the full spoon. "Isn't that how it always goes? You find the most unexpected item in the least likely spot. Was it hidden under a floor board or behind a fake wall?" Sherry's eyes were wide with anticipation.

Hannah laughed. "You have a healthy imagination, Sherry. No, nothing as glamorous as all that. It was in a box filled with old letters." Hannah moved away from the chowder table. "And I've learned there are other copies floating around but they are all a bit different. I'll be selling the original map."

Sherry clapped her hands together. "How exciting. I didn't expect to fall into the middle of a real live exciting mystery."

"Well, you could call it that, especially with the two murders."

Her eyes widened. "Are they connected?"

Hannah shrugged. "That's my guess. Excuse me, I have to say hello to more people." She finished the rest of her chowder and set the bowl down. It was too much of a risk to try to circulate and eat at the same time, she realized.

"Of course," Sherry said as she got in line for a lobster roll.

Before Hannah could make the rounds, Laura Masterson pulled on Hannah's arm. "I wasn't sure I was in the right place." She looked around the inside of the pub and wrinkled her nose. "It's a tad rundown compared to the rest of Hooks Harbor. When is the map event? I have a bit of money left from my father and I thought I'd invest it in the map. You know, in his memory. I feel like he's right here with me," she gushed.

Great, thought Hannah, almost laughing, a ghost to hang out with Great Aunt Caroline. Hannah had no feeling that her Great Aunt Caroline was sitting on her shoulder or whispering in her ear or in any way looking out for her. On the contrary, Great Aunt Caroline dumped this mess in Hannah's lap when she died and left it for her to figure out.

Maybe that was the point. Great Aunt Caroline had always been an independent person, taking the less traveled path, and loving it.

With the buried treasure map she forced Hannah to go out on a limb—be creative, brave, take control of her life, get out of her comfort zone. Was that the whole point? Hannah smiled to herself. Yeah, surprise,

surprise, just when she least expected it, Great Aunt Caroline *was* with her after all, pushing her to show everyone she could solve even the stickiest problem.

"What's the smile about, Ms. Holiday?" Hannah felt warm breath near her ear.

Hannah's smile vanished as quickly as it had appeared.

"I wouldn't suspect you would find anything to smile about with your sister and her daughter gone missing. But you could take me up on my offer to trade Caroline's property for them. Good deal, don't you think?"

Hannah slowly turned her head to look straight into Pearl's eyes. "I'll think about it."

Pearl laughed. "Nice bluff, dear." She checked her watch. "You have until Rocky gets back to win the treasure map." She moved toward Meg with a big smile as she paid for a lobster roll and bowl of clam chowder.

Meg caught Hannah's eye and silently mouthed, *poison it?* Hannah grinned and nodded before she turned away to mingle. She searched the crowd and spotted Cal's shaggy blond hair above most of the other patrons. She wormed her way through the crowd. As she approached, she heard the words *gold coins* and *jewelry*. If this didn't get the raffle tickets moving, nothing would, she thought.

Hannah tapped Cal's arm. He bent close to her face and asked, "How are you doing?"

"Pearl is here. She's acting very cocky, like she's holding all aces and expects me to fold at any minute, or at least by the time Rocky wins the map."

Cal's hand on the small of her back felt reassuring. "Let her keep thinking that." He pulled Hannah closer. "If Pearl is here, who's watching Ruby and Olivia?"

Hannah quickly scanned the crowd for Rocky's dark mop of hair. Nothing. Pearl and Rocky must have switched off to give

Pearl a chance to push Hannah's fear button a little harder.

"Call Ruby's phone. Now. She can outsmart that nit wit if he's the only one guarding her," Cal said as he pushed Hannah away from the crowd.

Without thinking, her fingers hit Ruby's number. The familiar loon call for Ruby's ring tone sounded not far from where she stood. Pearl caught Hannah's glance and answered. Hannah's shoulders sagged.

"You called, dear? Ready to make that deal?" Pearl held Ruby's phone to her ear. "It would have been an amateur mistake to leave Ruby's phone with Rocky. Don't worry, I know all the tricks." She disconnected the call and winked.

Hannah's phone rang. Her heart raced with anticipation. "Jack?"

She nodded and smiled before hanging up.

"What?" Cal asked.

She slid her phone into her front jeans pocket. "Pam's watching the house where Pearl took Ruby and Olivia. They appear to be safe for now. Pam's waiting for the right chance to rush in. Jack said to keep Pearl here. She's the devious one."

Chapter 20

Hannah found Michael and asked him for help.

"Sure thing." He snapped his fingers and two big, burly men appeared at Hannah's side. "Tell them what you need," Michael said before he moved away to help a customer.

Hannah felt dwarfed between Michael's friends. She described Pearl to them. "The old lady with purple hair," and explained their mission. "She can't leave. Do whatever it takes."

"You got an in with the cops? I don't want any jail time," the shorter guy with a nasty scar on his chin said.

"No worries. Just don't kill her. That's *my* reward," Hannah whispered.

Both men raised their eyebrows in shock before breaking into big grins. Scarface softly punched her shoulder. "Just like Caroline. Happy to be of service."

Hannah was impressed with how quickly they melted into the crowd and reappeared near Pearl. Scarface even chatted her up and must have told her a joke since she burst out laughing. Great.

Hannah called Jack. "Where are you? I want to see if I can help get Ruby and Olivia out."

Jack told her he would call Cal and give him the address. They could come together since Cal would know exactly where the house was. Pam wouldn't be happy, but Jack didn't care about that at the moment. Hannah checked with Meg and Michael to be sure everything was under control before heading off to find Cal.

"Go," Meg told Hannah. "Don't worry about a thing here. Just be back in time for the raffle winner."

Hannah had a brilliant idea. She got Scarface's attention and asked him if they could get Ruby's phone away from Pearl.

"Piece of cake. You wait by the door and I'll pass it to you in a few minutes."

By the time Hannah found Cal and checked that he had the address from Jack, Scarface brushed passed her, tucked Ruby's phone into her back pocket, and continued walking without skipping a stride. "Let's go," Hannah said to Cal as she stuck her thumb in her pocket to keep contact with the phone. "Time to rescue Ruby and Olivia."

Cal's truck bumped and bounced back down the dirt road. "How far is this house we're going to?" Hannah asked.

"After we pass your cottages, it's only a few miles."

As they neared her cottages, Hannah's arm reached across the front seat and hit Cal's arm. "Pull in. I need to get something." He swerved in next to Aaron's car.

"I'll wait here," Cal said.

Hannah quickly made a beeline to her cottage and stuffed a dark hooded sweatshirt and a baseball cap into a backpack. On her way back to the door, she saw Theodore sticking partway out from under her couch. She picked the well-loved bear up. "Poor Theodore. Olivia will be thrilled to see *you*." He got squished on top of the sweatshirt and she was out the door.

"Hannah? I didn't expect to see you here. Is the raffle over?"

"No, I have an errand to run before the winner is picked." Hannah strained her neck, searching between Aaron, Cottage Four, and his car. "Where's Laura?"

Aaron harumphed and shook his head. "You got her going with that buried treasure idea. I left her at the pub. She won't budge until, as she puts it, she wins the map. She's convinced her late father will somehow make sure *her* ticket is the winner."

"Are you convinced too?"

"Are you serious? I don't believe in that mumbo jumbo stuff, and I'm not thrilled she's *investing*," Aaron made big air quotes around investing, "the rest of her father's money. Dumb if you ask me. But she didn't ask and it's her money so I don't have any say in how she uses it." He placed a wicker basket in the back seat of his car and slammed the door. "We had a big argument about the whole thing." He stared into Hannah's face. "You know what the worst part is?"

Hannah shook her head.

"Sherry Wolfe is just as hyped up about this, and she encouraged Laura to go for the map. Sherry said, even if it doesn't pan out into much of a treasure, it'll make a wild story and Laura could sell it to some tabloid."

"Sell the treasure?"

Aaron puckered his lips. "No, the story. With photos. Sherry told Laura she knows *someone*," again he used air quotes, "to sell the story to. Laura would write about how we found the capsized boat, the murders, all the suspicious people in town, and the treasure map."

Cal honked the horn in his trunk. Hannah looked over at him and he motioned for her to hurry up. "I've got to go but I'm fascinated with this idea. Did Sherry say who she knows?"

"Naw. I doubt she knows anyone. She's just a retired school teacher with a big imagination and a nosy personality. I wish I hadn't been so friendly with her when she showed up with that gift basket for us." He pointed to the back seat. "A bunch of old snacks she probably cleaned out of her car and didn't want to throw out."

Hannah threw her backpack onto the seat of Cal's truck and jumped in next to it, slamming the door shut. "Let's go."

"What was that all about with Aaron?" Cal asked as he put the truck into reverse and drove away.

"He's frustrated with his wife for buying so many raffle tickets. And she has a new best friend, too."

"Who's that?"

"Sherry Wolfe. She's encouraging Laura to write a story about what's happened since they discovered the capsized boat. Sounds odd to me."

"What do you mean? You think Laura might have something to do with the murders?"

"Maybe. Looking back on the events, it seems odd how *they* found the boat first and Laura told me that her father had heard about this treasure. A strange coincidence or good planning to end up here at that moment?" Hannah shrugged. "It could be any of them." She stared at the passing scenery through the window. "But I'm leaning toward Pearl. She's had her fingers involved ever since Great Aunt Caroline asked her to help find Olivia's dad. And, as far as Pearl is concerned, the treasure she's after isn't buried in a sand dune somewhere; it's my property. She made *that* pretty clear."

"What's in your backpack?" Cal jiggled it.

"Clothes. I have a plan."

Cal parked his truck behind Jack's car, which was behind Pam's cruiser pulled into a hidden side street. Hannah grabbed the backpack and approached Pam who stood behind some trees. Without lowering her binoculars, she said, "Great. Draw more attention to me why don't you."

"It's my sister and niece and I've got a plan," Hannah stated without any friendly greeting.

Pam's arm fell to her side and she turned around, exhaling a huff. "I can't wait to hear this gem. Are you planning to waltz up to the front door and wait for someone to invite you in for tea and cookies?"

"Sort of. I'm going to use this," Hannah pulled Ruby's phone from her back pocket, "and pretend I'm Pearl calling to talk to Ruby."

"Why will Rocky think it's Pearl?"

Hannah held up the phone. "This is Ruby's phone. Rocky thinks Pearl has it, and with any luck, Pearl hasn't figured out she's lost it yet."

"I'm getting interested."

"Do you know the layout of the house?"

Pam nodded.

"Perfect. Is there a bathroom downstairs?"

Pam nodded again.

"Once I get Ruby on the phone, I'll tell her to take Olivia and go in the bathroom. I'll climb through the window and swap places with her. It won't take Rocky too long to figure it out but it should buy us enough time to get Ruby and Olivia to safety."

"So, they kill you instead," Pam said with sarcasm dripping from her words.

"No, Pearl needs me alive to get what she wants. Ruby and Olivia are her bargaining chips. Plus, I'm pretty sure I can put enough doubt in Rocky's brain to convince him to let me go."

"Okay. My first concern is getting Olivia to safety. If you want to jump into the fire for her, go ahead."

Hannah pulled the hooded sweatshirt over her head and coiled her hair under the baseball cap. She checked the phone for recent calls and hit Rocky's number.

"Yeah, Pearl?" Hannah was relieved to hear Rocky's voice. The first step in her plan was sound.

"Put Ruby on." Hannah kept to as few words as possible and spoke quickly. She held her breath until she heard Ruby's voice. "Pearl?"

Hannah spoke softly into the phone, "Listen and stay calm. Take Olivia into the bathroom, turn on the water, and open the window. I'm coming in to trade places with you. Say, *okay Pearl*, and hang up."

Hannah heard Ruby's words and the phone line was disconnected. The last thing Hannah did was tuck Theodore safely under her arm before she followed the tree line along the side of the property.

Once she could see the open window, she sprinted to the house, staying as low to the ground as possible. The window was higher than she could comfortably reach. Panic set in until she saw a patio chair nearby. Dragging it under the window, she stepped up and felt Ruby's hands grab her arms and pull her through into the bathroom. Hannah quickly pulled her hat and sweatshirt off, trading for Ruby's hat and zippered fleece.

Hannah nestled Theodore into Olivia's arms. She crouched down and talked face to face to Olivia. "You need to keep him safe. Be quiet and do exactly what Mommy says."

Olivia, her eyes wide with the big responsibility Hannah bestowed on her, nodded solemnly.

"Nice choice of clothes," Ruby said as she pulled Hannah's dark sweatshirt over her head.

"It will help you blend in with the trees." A quick hug and Ruby went out the window feet first. Hannah lowered Olivia and Theodore down to Ruby's outstretched arms.

Hannah watched Ruby until she disappeared into the trees. She sat on the edge of the tub. That part went easier than expected, but now what?

A loud knock on the door and Rocky's voice brought Hannah back to her situation. "You okay in there?"

"Olivia's trying to poop. We'll be a bit longer I'm afraid." Hannah was confident that Rocky wouldn't be able to hear any difference between Hannah's and Ruby's voices. They were always confused on the phone growing up.

She heard Rocky mutter, "Geesh, too much information."

Hannah smiled to herself with that quick response that bought her some time. She forced her breathing to slow.

Ruby's phone rang. "This isn't good," Hannah said as the distinctive loon call sounded again.

"Hey." The bathroom door rattled. "Open up. I hear that crazy phone ringing."

Hannah looked at the phone, angry with herself for forgetting to silence the ringer. This wasn't part of the plan. What was she going to do next? She really didn't think it through beyond getting Ruby and Olivia out. Should she run for it, too?

A loud crash sent the door splintering at the hinges. Rocky held a phone to his ear. "They got away, Nana. Looks like we got the big prize instead. She climbed right into the trap like you predicted." Hannah's stomach clenched at the sight of Rocky's lopsided grin.

Chapter 21

"You'll never get away with this, you know." Hannah kept her voice calm and soothing—while her insides twisted into knots—hoping she could find a crack in Rocky's defenses.

He smiled and motioned for her to come out of the bathroom. "Don't be so sure, Doll Face. Nana's a sharp cookie. Don't underestimate her." He patted Hannah's pockets and found both phones—hers and Ruby's. "You won't be needing these."

"What's your plan with me, Rocky? Surely, Pearl can't be thinking of killing me like she did Marco and Lenny."

"Sit over there." He pointed to a couch against a wall away from any windows. "And keep quiet. I need to think."

Hannah made sure to walk as close to the picture window as possible. She assumed Pam still had her binoculars trained on the house. She wanted them to know she was okay. At least for the moment.

"Why does Pearl want my property, Rocky?"

He scowled when his eyes met hers. "What are you blabbering about?"

"The cottages and snack bar. What are her plans with the property?"

"We're after the map to find that buried treasure. She didn't tell me nothin' about no property." Rocky sank into a soft chair. "She told me to buy up as many raffle tickets as possible, but then she told me to come here." He shrugged. "I guess her plan changed."

"Without telling you? That doesn't sound like a plan that you're a valuable part of."

"Yeah. You've got a point. Why would she do that?" He ran both hands through his dark, wavy hair.

"Is she going to let you have the buried treasure and she's taking the big prize? The ocean front property?" Hannah let that sink in before hitting Rocky with the real shocker. "That buried treasure? I'm not convinced it even exists."

Rocky stood up quickly. "You're selling the map. Are you scamming everyone?" Anger burned in his eyes.

Hannah sat forward and held up both hands. "I'm raffling off a map I found in my Great Aunt Caroline's papers. And for a good cause, in case you forgot. I won't benefit from it. I never made any promise about what anyone might find from following the map, though. This whole thing took on a life of its own, starting with that boating accident." She leaned back and forced herself to relax and talk with a soothing voice. "What can you tell me about that, Rocky? About the boating accident involving Marco and Lenny?"

Rocky paced around the small living room. "Marco botched that up royally," he muttered more to himself than to Hannah. "Nana was furious." He spun around and glared at Hannah. "After Lenny led everyone to your doorstep, Marco was supposed to get rid of that dope once and for all and find the treasure."

"What happened?"

"Nana should never have trusted that slimy investigator." He punched his right fist into the palm of his left hand. "But, no, she refused to listen to me. Lenny left his bags at your place. How stupid was that?"

"Completely foolish. Lenny couldn't disappear without a trace with all that evidence under my nose."

Rocky whipped around. "Exactly. You get it, but Nana wouldn't listen to me."

"That upsets you, doesn't it, Rocky? Pearl has to do things her way, doesn't she?"

"That's why she can't stay married. *She* has to be the boss." He scowled. "What should I do?"

"I don't know." Hannah realized this could be a tricky question. She had to *lead* Rocky to his own conclusions instead of *telling* him what to do like everyone else. "What if you call Pearl and try to find out what she's *really* up to?"

"Yeah. Good idea." He pulled out his phone and dialed. He scowled. "She's not answering."

Hannah held her hand out. "Let me try. With Ruby's phone." Hannah's heart beat so hard she thought it might burst through her chest.

Rocky hesitated. "All right." He held the phone out but pulled it back as Hannah reached for it. "No funny business," he said before he finally gave her the phone.

Hannah made a quick decision and hit Pam's number instead. If Rocky heard her answer, at least she might sound like Pearl from where he stood across the room. "What?" Pam's voice rang loud and clear in Hannah's ear.

"Listen, Pearl," Hannah blurted out. "Rocky's bringing me to the pub. He said I need to be there for the drawing so people don't get suspicious." Hannah kept her eyes on Rocky's face and relaxed slightly when the edge of his mouth twitched up into a grin. He nodded and gave her two thumbs up. She nodded with the phone tight against her ear. "Yeah. That's right."

Hannah slipped the phone in her own pocket at the same time she gave Rocky the message. "Pearl said she'll talk to you when you get me there. She said it's a *smart* idea."

Rocky's face broke into a big smile. "Smart, huh? It's about time she gives me some credit. Let's go, Doll Face."

Hannah let out a deep silent exhale. She could relax. Rocky took her story hook, line, and sinker. Now she only had to get back to the pub without Pam interfering. Pam's words on the phone to Hannah were—*I hope you know what you're doing.* Hannah had the same thought.

Rocky led the way. He stopped suddenly and Hannah smacked right into his back. She stepped sideways and peeked around to see what happened. This might be interesting, she thought.

Rocky looked at Hannah. "What are *they* doing here? Haven't these two been staying at your cottages?"

Hannah nodded her head. "Yeah, but I have no idea why they're here. Just play it cool and ask them what they want. Or do you want me to talk to them?"

He used his elbow to push Hannah in front of him. "You talk to them. They're your guests."

Laura slid out of the driver's side of her car. "We watched you sneak away from the pub and decided to follow you. It got pretty exciting when you climbed through the window."

Sherry stepped from the passenger side. "Yeah, you know, follow the trail to the money, or buried treasure in this case." She giggled.

"Sorry to disappoint you two sleuths, but I'm heading back to the pub right now. Where's Aaron?"

Laura flicked her wrist dismissively. "He's not interested in the buried treasure like," she glanced at Sherry, "we are. He decided to take a walk on the beach instead."

Right, Hannah thought. "You left him at the cottages? How do you know he's not searching for the treasure on his own?" She smiled with satisfaction when both their faces fell. "Maybe you'd better get back and keep an eye on him."

Rocky finally found his voice. "Let's all stick together. I don't like the idea of anyone stealing that treasure away from me. Come on. You two in my car with Doll Face."

Doll Face? Hannah saw Laura mouth the name to Sherry. They both covered their mouths.

"I better grab my tote," Laura giggled.

When she opened the back door, Rocky's eyes lit up. "Are those snacks? I'm starving."

Laura handed the basket to Rocky. "Help yourself." She slung her canvas tote over her shoulder and slid into the backseat of Rocky's car. "My girlfriends aren't gonna believe this cloak and dagger stuff," she said to Sherry. "And if I win the buried treasure?" She squealed with excitement.

Rocky dropped the basket on Hannah's lap after he dug around and came up with some peanut butter cups. "Want anything, Doll Face?"

Hannah shook her head. Her stomach was tied in knots. She wasn't going to send any high fat snacks down to turn the knots into cement blocks. What did she get herself into? Any of these three people could be a killer. Although the way Laura was acting like such a ninny, Hannah doubted whether she could have committed cold blooded murder. Twice.

She let her hand rest on her pocket with Ruby's phone. At least she might have a chance to get a call off in an emergency. With that thought, the phone rang. Silence fell inside the car.

"It must be Pearl. Answer it," Rocky ordered.

"Pearl?" Hannah let herself breathe when she heard Pam's voice ask her what was going on. "Yeah, we're on our way, Pearl. Wait for us at the pub." Hannah put the phone away from ear and whispered to Rocky, "Want me to tell her anything else?"

"Yeah. Tell her I'm expecting her to tell me all the details about Marco and Lenny. I don't plan to take the rap for something she did."

Hannah relayed the message. She hesitated before she hit disconnect, wanting to keep the call on speaker phone, but that could be too risky. Laura giggled in the back seat and Sherry talked nonstop about how much money they would get for this story.

"It'll be *huge*," Sherry said. "Especially with the photos you have."

Hannah turned around and looked at Laura in the backseat. "Photos?"

"Yeah. Here, take a look." She handed her phone to Hannah.

Hannah scanned through Laura's photos of the capsized boat, something floating in the water, Rocky digging holes, and even Hannah climbing through the bathroom window. Some tabloid would blow the photos up and have a field day with them. Great, Hannah groaned. Her butt might end up on the front page of some daily rag. "Did you show these to the police?" Hannah asked Laura.

"Of course not! Sherry told me to keep them secret if I want to make some money off them." Sherry grabbed the phone back.

Rocky tried to pull into the Pub and Pool Hall parking lot. It was still packed. He had to back up and park on the side of the road leading to the pub. Hannah craned her neck around. Where were Pam and Cal, she wondered. Didn't they follow Rocky? She really was hoping for some reinforcements, especially once Rocky found out that she hadn't actually talked to Pearl. Well, with all these people around, at least Hannah felt safer.

"Let's go, Doll Face. Almost time to pull out that winning raffle ticket. I can feel it. I know I've got the winner." Rocky pumped his fist in the air for emphasis.

"Not so fast, big guy," Laura said. "I've got the winner. Me and Sherry went in on a lot of tickets together."

"Oh yeah? Where are *your* tickets?" Rocky asked, his fingers twitching with anticipation.

Laura held up her canvas tote covered with bright red lobsters but Sherry tried to pull it away. "Don't show him, you fool."

Too late. Rocky reached for the bag but Laura spun away from him. Sherry grabbed it from Laura and ran toward the pub, clutching the precious bag under her arm. Rocky chased after Sherry, catching her and one strap of the tote that hung down. They each pulled but the stitching on the cloth bag couldn't handle the stress. Raffle tickets fluttered around Rocky's and

Sherry's feet. Laura screeched, "All my tickets."

Ruby, Pam, and Cal caught up with Hannah as she leaned on Rocky's car. "Where'd the rest of your gang disappear to in such a hurry?" Pam asked.

Hannah pointed to the three stooges just outside the pub door, shoving each other as they tried to scoop up the scattered raffle tickets. "Serves them right," Hannah said.

A red Mazda Miata with the top down streaked out of the parking lot. "I wonder where Pearl's going in such a hurry," Hannah said.

"She won't get far. I have a roadblock set up to get her for kidnapping Ruby and Olivia," Pam said.

"What about murder?" Hannah asked.

"Maybe that, too. But if it's not her, I'm keeping an eye on those others." Pam took long strides toward the pub.

Suddenly, Hannah grabbed Ruby's arm. "Where's Olivia?"

"Jack took her to his house. She was ready for some food and a nap. I wanted to make sure you were all right." Ruby wrapped her arms around Hannah and squeezed her until she gasped. "Thanks for putting your life on the line for us. I don't think Rocky was planning to hurt us, but I wasn't sure about Pearl. She's crazy."

Chapter 22

The sound of sirens filled Hannah's ears like it was music.

"I don't think we'll have to worry about Pearl. The police must have that crazy, purple-haired lady in handcuffs." Hannah's stomach growled. She pulled out the gift basket from the front seat of Rocky's car and held it in the air. "Anyone want a snack?"

Cal's eyes lit up. "Sure, what have you got in there?"

Hannah tipped the basket over onto the hood of Rocky's car. "I don't think Laura will mind. Her husband said it was a bunch of stale stuff from Sherry."

Ruby pushed the pile of snacks around and sorted them—chocolate candy, sugary fruity candy, peppermints, and various packages of crackers. Absentmindedly, she opened a bag of chocolate candies and popped a handful in her mouth. She stuffed a couple more bags in her pocket. "For Olivia," she explained.

"Sure," Hannah teased. "I know you and your chocolate addiction."

"And what about your peanut butter obsession?" Ruby responded as she pushed several packages of peanut butter crackers into Hannah's pocket.

"Leave some for me," Cal said. He took something from each pile. "I like it all."

The country music that had been blaring through the outside speakers suddenly went quiet. Cal pushed both Hannah and Ruby away from the junk food. "We'd better get inside. It's almost time for the drawing."

"If nothing else, I hope we raised a lot of money for the library," Hannah said on their way inside.

"And, here she is, Hannah Holiday." Michael's voice raised above all the chatter in the pub. "Our own keeper of the buried treasure map. Will you do the honors?"

Michael held up a huge clear jug stuffed full of the raffle tickets.

As Hannah moved through the crowd, Rocky quickly leaned toward her and whispered, "No funny stuff, Doll Face."

Hannah shot him a glare and kept walking to the bar. Michael pointed to a stool for her to stand on so everyone could see what was happening. Hoots and hollers erupted from around the pub. "Most excitement in Hooks Harbor since Caroline accidentally, as she said, ran into Chase Fuller's pride and joy with her little dinghy." Someone else laughed. "Yeah, she put a hole right through the back and it sank so fast Chase had to swim to shore. Lucky for him, she didn't run him over." A group of locals laughed so hard Hannah thought they might spray their beer all over everyone standing near them.

"Okay, then." Hannah tried to get the attention of the crowd back on the raffle tickets. She stuck her hand into the jug and stirred it around until she felt one ticket that she decided should be the winner. She pulled it out and held it over her head. "Is everyone ready?"

She paused before reading the number. "The winning ticket is 312268."

From the back of the pub, one of the locals held his arm up. "I don't believe it," he yelled. "I've never won anything before."

Hannah recognized Pete, Michael's friend, who rescued them after Meg's tire blew out. She smiled to herself, glad that one of the locals was the winner. And, someone big and bulky enough to intimidate Rocky if he got any crooked ideas about taking the map for himself.

Meg handed Hannah a slip of paper. Hannah held her hand up. "Don't leave yet. Thank you all for helping raise twenty five hundred dollars for the Hooks Harbor Library. In addition to a generous one thousand dollar donation," Hannah glanced quickly at Rocky's scowling face, "the raffle raised an additional fifteen hundred dollars."

Cal climbed up next to Hannah. "Don't forget about the delicious food you all enjoyed here today. Hannah's snack bar should be open for business as soon as the final inspection is done. Today was a tease for your taste buds. Make sure to stop by and see what else she'll be serving."

The floor was littered with discarded raffle tickets. The crowd got back to their conversations, pool playing, drinking, and eating.

Pete approached Hannah. He timidly gave her a big bear hug. She pulled the map from her pocket, chuckling that Rocky never even looked for it when he found her after she snuck through the bathroom window.

Pete refused to take the map from Hannah. "Nope. I don't even want the map. I like the *idea* of a buried treasure. It's much more exciting to wonder what it is. I bet Caroline buried a bunch of old shells or something like that anyway."

Hannah was speechless. After all the drama, greed, and murder connected to the map, here was someone who couldn't care less about it. She shook her head and squeezed Pete's arm. "Maybe we'll raffle it off again next year. I'm sure the library can always use donations."

Hannah checked the time. She was tired. She scanned the room looking for Cal or someone to give her a ride back to her cottages.

"That was exciting," Sherry said, sidling up next to Hannah. "And the best part? You still have the map. What a generous guy the winner is." She stood quietly next to Hannah for a minute. "Are you looking for someone?"

Hannah sighed. "I am. Suddenly I'm exhausted and I need a ride back to my cottages."

"I'm heading that way myself. I'd be happy to give you a ride." Sherry smiled.

Hannah followed Sherry to her car. She wondered where Cal and Ruby disappeared to. Oh well, they'd figure out that she left. Sherry moved her backpack and another box from the passenger seat to the backseat to make room for Hannah. "There you go. Make yourself comfortable."

Sherry chatted away as they drove. Hannah tuned out the words, responding with a yes or a nod at, what she hoped, were the appropriate places. She pulled out one of the packages of crackers and idly munched on them, wishing she had eaten more of Meg's delicious food instead of this stale peanut butter cracker.

Hannah pointed. "Watch out for the pothole."

Sherry swerved but it was too late and her little car jerked to one side as everything on her back seat slid to the floor. Hannah turned around to rescue Sherry's things. The box had tipped over, spilling its contents behind Hannah's seat.

Hannah reached back and the cracker wrapper slipped from her fingers, landing next to a set of knives. One was missing. Hannah's heart flipped and flopped. Where had she seen them before?

"Oh dear," Sherry said. "I'd better clean that mess up." She pulled over to the side of the road. Hannah didn't wipe the fear from her face quickly enough. Sherry looked at Hannah's face, then at the items on the floor.

"Well, well, well. That wasn't part of my plan," Sherry said matter-of-factly, losing her chatty, friendly voice. She reached back and picked up one of the knives. "Now, what will I do?" She flicked her fingernail over the point of the knife blade. "Such a shame to waste another one of these."

"You murdered Marco and Lenny? Why?"

"Oh, Hannah. You haven't figured it out yet? No, of course you haven't. You kept looking in the wrong direction. Pearl and her grandson gave you enough drama to make you suspect them, didn't they?"

"You'll never get away with it, Sherry."

"Why not? A retired school teacher? Besides, I heard the police have Pearl in custody and she'll probably blame her grandson to save her own skin. By the time anyone finds you, I'll be long gone. Oh, that reminds me, hand over the map. After all, that *is* what this was all about."

Hannah pulled the map from her pocket. "It's a hoax. There isn't a treasure."

Sherry scowled. "What are you talking about?"

"The map. It was a scheme to get tourists to come to Hooks Harbor." Hannah shrugged. "It worked. People came, spent their money at the local restaurants and other businesses. Turns out it was a treasure for the whole town."

Sherry ripped the map from Hannah's hand. "I don't believe you. Marco and Lenny planned this for months."

"How did you fit into the picture, Sherry?" Hannah was surprised at how calm her voice sounded to her own ears while her brain raced through every escape avenue she could think of.

"I convinced Lenny I would help him once Marco was out of the way. He wasn't keen on me helping but he did need *someone*. I brought Lenny dry clothes and snacks after he made it to shore. He hid in the woods until the coast was clear and," she shrugged her shoulders, "the rest is history. He was an easy target when he tried to sneak under your snack bar when he thought I was asleep."

"Clever."

"Yup. Now get out," Sherry ordered as she stood by the driver's side of the car. "My side of the car. Time to get this show on the road." She kept the knife pointed at Hannah only inches away from her neck.

Hannah slowly slid by the steering wheel. She took the keys, thinking they might be useful as a weapon if Sherry let her guard down. Sherry backed up just enough to make room for Hannah to slide out the door. With the knife blade pressed against Hannah's neck, Sherry grabbed Hannah's arm and twisted it behind her back. "There, just in case you were thinking of taking off."

Now Hannah was beginning to panic. Sherry's grip was like an iron vice and the knife was beginning to dig deeper into her skin.

"Move. Into the woods." Sherry pushed Hannah from behind.

Hannah planted her feet but Sherry poked the knife deeper into her neck. Hannah felt a sharp pain and a trickle of something warm run down her neck and under her shirt.

She could hear a truck approaching. She had to stay in sight. Sherry poked her again and whispered in her ear. "Move, or I'll push the knife all the way in right now."

Hannah jabbed her free elbow around and connected with Sherry's chest. She raked the keys across Sherry's face. Sherry screamed and covered her face with her arms. The knife flew away into the road just as Pete's truck, with Cal and Ruby, stopped next to them. Pete sprang into action. He pulled Sherry away from Hannah. Before Hannah could even turn around, Pete had Sherry on the ground with his knee on her back. It all happened in seconds.

Ruby had her arms around her sister, and Cal embraced them both.

Ruby sobbed. "When Meg told me she saw you leave with Sherry, I got a flashback of the peanut butter cracker wrappers." She stared into Hannah's eyes. "It was Sherry all along, wasn't it? Clever-friendly-chatty-afraid-of-Petunia, Sherry."

Hannah nodded.

Cal pulled the braid away from Hannah's neck and stared at the blood. "What happened?"

"She held a knife to my neck to make me walk into the woods so she could finish me off. Pete got here just in time."

Pam's cruiser screeched to a stop in the middle of the road. "Nice work, Pete. I'll take her from here." She looked at Hannah and shook her head. "Was this part of your plan, too? I'm not sure I would have played it so close to the edge."

Cal helped Hannah into the back seat of Pete's truck. "Ready to go home?"

Hannah leaned her head on his shoulder. "Yes."

Jack and Olivia were waiting for them to arrive. Olivia was beside herself with excitement. "Pearl left and didn't take Petunia." Her eyes were big and round. "I already told her she could stay here with Hannah and Nellie."

Hannah smiled. "Of course she can." After all, there was no way Petunia could stay with Pearl in jail.

Chapter 23

Laura and Aaron stopped in to say goodbye. Laura couldn't believe she had befriended a killer. "I guess that's a good ending seeing as I didn't win the treasure map," she said to Aaron as they walked to their car. "My friends aren't going to believe what happened on our honeymoon."

Meg arrived with clam chowder, cole slaw, and lobster salad. "In case anyone is hungry," she said as she covered Hannah's table with food.

Finally, Hannah thought, delicious food and a chance to relax. Pearl and Rocky were locked up for kidnapping and Sherry wouldn't be seeing the light of day for a long time.

She groaned when she heard a knock on her door.

Jack opened it. A man in a business suit holding a packet of papers said he was looking for Olivia Holiday.

Ruby and Hannah shared their look.

"Can I come in?" he asked politely.

Ruby nodded, Jack moved aside, and the man entered. "Olivia Holiday is the sole heir of Lenny DiMarco's estate."

Olivia was sitting on Ruby's lap. "This is Olivia. I'm her mother, Ruby. I don't understand what this is all about."

The man handed Ruby a sheet of paper. She skimmed it. Caroline Holiday's signature jumped off the page as the witness for the Last Will and Testament of Lenny DiMarco.

"I don't believe this, Hannah." Ruby waved the paper through the air. "This is the real treasure. Caroline found Lenny and made sure he did the right thing for his daughter." Ruby looked at the man. "What will she get?"

"A lot. Here's my card. Come to my office next week and I'll show you everything. Lenny DiMarco was a very wealthy man."

Hannah's grin spread across her face. She looked at Ruby who sat with her arms around Olivia, her eyes blinking, and tears streaming down her cheeks.

The End

A Note from Lyndsey

Thank you for reading my cozy mystery, *Mobsters and Lobsters.*

If you enjoyed this book in the Hooked & Cooked Cozy Mystery Series, be sure to join my FREE COZY MYSTERY BOOK CLUB! Be in the know for new releases, promotions, sales, and the possibility to receive advanced reader copies. Join the club here—http://LyndseyColeBooks.com

ABOUT THE AUTHOR

Lyndsey Cole lives in New England in a small rural town with her husband who puts up with all the characters in her head, her dog who hogs the couch, her cat who is the boss, and 3 chickens that would like to move into the house. She surrounds herself with gardens full of beautiful perennials. Sitting among the flowers with the scent of lilac, peonies, lily of the valley, or whatever is in bloom, stimulates her imagination about who will die next!

OTHER BOOKS BY LYNDSEY COLE

The Hooked & Cooked Series

Gunpowder Chowder

The Black Cat Café Series

BlueBuried Muffins

StrawBuried in Chocolate

BlackBuried Pie

Very Buried Cheesecake

RaspBuried Torte

PoisonBuried Punch

CranBuried Coffee Cake

The Lily Bloom Series

Begonias Mean Beware

Queen of Poison

Roses are Dead

Drowning in Dahlias

Hidden by the Hydrangeas

Christmas Tree Catastrophe

Made in the USA
Middletown, DE
16 September 2021